"If you don't wish your reputation to be ruined quite beyond repair, why did you drag a perfect stranger into your bedchamber?"

"You were well on your way to ruining my reputation without any help from me, my lord," she replied, anger deepening her voice and bringing out a hint of Irish roots. "You couldn't possibly have come up with an explanation for your presence in my room that would have satisfied that man. I don't know who he is and clearly you don't either. Let him go on thinking, therefore, that we are man and wife. We'll never see him again and no harm done."

"That's all very well," Christopher retorted, unwilling to consider that she might have a point. "But in the meantime, I'm stuck here in your bedroom!"

"Well, I'm very sorry, but I'll try not to take advantage of you."

Christopher could see that as soon as the words were spoken she regretted them. A deep crimson stained her cheeks and her hand came up to cover her mouth, presumably before any more unfortunate phrases could escape. Her eyes widened, and he saw for the first time that they were the deep blue of an evening's ocean with stars twinkling like sapphires in their luminous depths. He felt a twinge of satisfaction at the unexpectedness. He also noticed that she was younger than he had suspected when she seemed so eminently self-assured. In fact…he refused to allow his thoughts to travel any further. This was not the time.

Even if it most assuredly was the place.

Counterfeit Viscountess

by

Barbara Burke

This is a work of fiction. Names, characters, places, and incidents are either the product of the author's imagination or are used fictitiously, and any resemblance to actual persons living or dead, business establishments, events, or locales, is entirely coincidental.

Counterfeit Viscountess

Cover Art by *Abigail Owen*

The Wild Rose Press, Inc.
PO Box 708
Adams Basin, NY 14410-0708
Visit us at www.thewildrosepress.com

Publishing History
First Tea Rose Edition, 2020
Print ISBN 978-1-5092-3112-6
Digital ISBN 978-1-5092-3113-3

Published in the United States of America

Dedication

Always to Ross

Chapter One

It was late and Christopher Hawkins had spent the better part of the evening performing an unpleasant task that had taken far longer than it should. He was tired, angry and impatient, as much with himself as with the nincompoop behind the bar at the Hare and Hound. He ached all over and wanted a hot bath, a bottle of brandy and a bed. In that precise order, with no omissions or substitutions. If he couldn't make the man see reason, none of his requirements would be fulfilled. The very thought made him even more tired and angry. Not to mention impatient.

It was clear, however, that no amount of impatience or anger would serve to provide him with a room, despite the fact that he had sent word of his projected arrival well in advance. The nincompoop, who was called Bob when no one was angry with him, just smiled apologetically and continued to bleat some nonsense about there being no room available.

Christopher took a deep breath, preparing to blast Bob into both finding him a room and next week. His tirade was forestalled, however, by the sudden appearance of Bob's employer, Tom Stafford, the owner of the Hare and Hounds, wearing an anxious expression on his usually jovial face. Upon seeing who was creating the ruckus his face broke into smiles.

"Lord Saxon! How good to see you again," he

exclaimed, before turning a more forbidding expression on his luckless assistant. "What is the problem here? Why is Lord Saxon being kept standing around like a common stagecoach passenger? Escort him to a room at once," he commanded.

"That's just it, sir. As I was trying to explain to the gentleman, there isn't a room to be had. Not anywhere, neither upstairs nor down. The last room's been took long since."

"And as I was just trying to explain to this…fellow, I booked a room, and if someone has mistakenly been given it in my stead they must be informed and moved forthwith," Christopher said, his teeth clenched and his eyes daring anyone to disagree with him.

"I'm sure it's just a misunderstanding, my lord," the proprietor replied, his manner both conciliatory and respectful. "We'll have it sorted out in jig time. Now then, Bob, what has happened to the room Lord Saxon requested?"

"I don't know, sir. All the rooms are taken, including Lord Saxon's. Here, see for yourself." He eagerly handed over the book the generally efficient staff used to keep track of the comings and goings of their guests.

Stafford carefully rooted through the pocket of his jacket and then placed a pair of spectacles on the edge of his nose before taking charge of the book. He looked at the open page carefully for several minutes, driving Christopher almost to distraction before looking up with a smile.

"Well, my lord, it's clear to me a mistake has been made. Here's your name and here's the number of the best room in the inn beside it all right and tight and arranged for this evening's hire. But someone's written it down as occupied, which it clearly isn't since you're standing here before me now having only just arrived. If you'd like to step into the salon and warm yourself with a glass of brandy, as my guest, of course. I'll nip upstairs with your bags and make sure everything is set to rights. Bob, you show his lordship into the salon and pour him a glass of the best."

"Thank you, Mr. Stafford. I'm travelling light, so you need not worry about my luggage. I'll accept your offer of a glass of brandy with good will and warm myself before your excellent fire after the journey. Then I'd like to get out of all my dirt. Please send a tub and some hot water up. I need a good long soak."

"Ahhh." For the first time the proprietor looked nonplussed. "Now that's something that's not so easily arranged, I'm afraid. Our Nellie being off to her sister's to help with her lie-in, we're a mite short staffed and making do with a girl from the village. I've agreed to allow her to go home of an evening, and it being so late, there's neither hot water nor person to bring it up. I'm sorry, my lord, but I'm afraid there's no help for it. There won't be any way to have a bath before morning."

"Fine," Christopher said shortly, a sudden weariness overtaking him at this final impediment. "As long as the brandy is up to your usual standards."

The proprietor's anxious face broke into a smile. "That, my lord, I can assure you of."

It wasn't until he settled in front of the rekindled fire in the salon that Christopher realized just how tired he was. Home from an extensive sojourn on the continent only a matter of hours he had been forced by the tearful pleas of his sister to drop everything to rush to the rescue of a nephew who was as defiant as he was ungrateful. He had arrived yesterday at a small village church just in the nick of time to stop a marriage as ill-omened as it was ill-conceived. The young groom, far from being thankful for an intervention that could only save him from a lifetime of regret, instead ripped up at his uncle for ruining his life. When it was pointed out that at eighteen he couldn't very well be considered to know what would and would not ruin his life, he was furious enough to take an ill-advised swing at his savior. The blow did not land, but it tried Christopher's temper to its limits and quenched any secret sympathy he might have felt for the young lovers.

After dragging his nephew to an indifferent inn where he spent the night guarding against any rash attempt on the young man's part to reunite with his erstwhile bride, he spent the next day negotiating with the young swain's prospective father-in-law to prevent an action for breach of promise being brought. The ruthless tactics used by the bride's father, cut short only by Christopher's final assurance that his nephew was underage and, therefore, not to be held responsible for any contract he may or may not have entered into, cleared a lot of the stars out of the boy's eyes. The few left were routed by the eager way the outrageous amount of money his uncle impatiently agreed to settle on the heartbroken miss—and her father—was accepted as more than making up for the alienation of his affections on the part of both bride and father. It was a sadder, but, Christopher hoped, wiser young man who was finally taken back to Oxford and told in no uncertain terms to keep his nose clean until the end of term or face consequences that would devastate both his pocketbook and his pride.

Christopher, meanwhile, was left to travel back to London and assure his widowed sister that her only son was safe. Or at least that this particular crisis had been successfully vanquished. He could only shudder to think what the sprig would get up to next. Fortunately, he was quite fond of both mother and child, though he would be unlikely to admit it at the moment, and dragging young Michael out of trouble, and reassuring the boy's mother that he had done so, had become second nature. So, despite the fact that his business had been dropped higgledy-piggledy back into his bailiff's hands, he never considered turning west and allowing his sister to hear of her son's deliverance by post. He would have to go to London and reassure her in person. But it had been a long few days of rapid travel in an equipage that wasn't meant for such distances, and he ached with weariness.

Finding himself dropping off before the warmth of the fire, he decided to forego the rest of the admittedly excellent brandy and take himself off to bed. He downed the last of his glass and went in search of his bag, which he found sitting beside the counter in the taproom. Quietly making his way up the stairs, he realized for the first time how late it was. One or two voices could be heard emanating from behind closed doors, but all was darkness beyond the windows and the light he carried with him.

He had stayed at the inn before and knew the location of the room he had been assigned. He had some difficulty with the latch and cursed softly at the ill-fitting mechanism of the lock. Apparently, it wasn't softly enough. As he fiddled with the fixture, the door across the hallway opened and a suspicious face peered around the aged oak to see what the commotion was.

"Sorry to disturb you," Christopher said quietly. "My door seems to be stuck."

The man's glance travelled carefully from Christopher's rather the worse for wear high top boots to his disarranged cravat and tousled hair. The expensive attire and confident air that Christopher wore as naturally as his birthright helped to abate the suspicious look on the man's face, but he didn't appear completely reassured

"Can't be too careful at this time of night," he said. "Don't know what kinds of rogues might be about searching for easy pickings from weary travellers."

"I assure you, sir, whatever kind of rogue I may be I'm not the sort looking for easy pickings, merely my bed for the night. Now if you'll excuse me…" He felt a foolish reluctance to wrestle with the door under the watchful eye of his interrogator. Drawing himself up to his full six feet, he continued: "My name is Christopher Hawkins, Viscount Saxon. If you wish to continue this conversation perhaps we could do so in the morning."

The man gave him another long look before relaxing. "No offense intended, my lord. Just being careful." With a short nod, he pulled his head back in and firmly closed the door to his room.

A determined push with his shoulder solved Christopher's problem with his own door and he found himself propelled into the room a little more precipitately than he had intended. He bit back another curse.

The light from his candle showed that the fire had

almost completely died out, a bed of shimmering orange coals the only sign of life in the grate. The basket on the hearth still contained a few chopped logs and he crossed the room toward it, determined to build up a blaze to see him comfortably through the remainder of the night.

As he placed the last piece of wood on the fire, he heard rustling from the bed that lay in shadows behind him.

"Is that you, Annie?" a husky voice asked sleepily.

Christopher froze, his hand still outstretched toward the blaze. What the devil was a woman doing in his bed? Especially a half-asleep woman who possessed the kind of voice clearly made for subdued firelight and the privacy of a bedroom. Unfortunately, it was also clearly a voice whose owner was expecting a very different person to respond to her enquiry. Any wild fleeting thoughts of manna from heaven were quickly banished, replaced by a burning desire to flee before the entire house and a terrible scandal were brought down upon his unwitting shoulders.

The thought was given no opportunity to become deed. The woman in the bed suddenly sat up in apparent confusion, pulling the quilt up around her organza-clad shoulders and peering toward the light of the fire as it threw Christopher's silhouette into sharp relief.

"Who's there?" she asked, a sudden sharpness chasing the sleep from her voice. "What are you doing?"

Christopher's first thought was one of relief that she didn't seem to be the hysterical type. A screaming woman in his bed was the last thing he needed.

"I'm very sorry," he said quietly, looking away as best he could from the flickering planes of the woman's shape under the covers. He stood up slowly, careful to make no move that could be construed as threatening, to stay as far away from the bed as possible. "I believe there has been some mistake. I was told this room was unoccupied. I had reserved it for myself earlier and clearly would not have entered had I realized someone was already in possession."

The woman, though roused from a deep sleep and understandably confused, did not leap to the obvious reaction. She studied the man carefully for a long minute, trying to get her bearings, before responding.

"In that case, perhaps you would be kind enough to leave immediately."

"Certainly," Christopher replied, the relief in his voice patent.

He had just reached his hand out to gently turn the handle when her voice once again pulled him up.

"Wait." The command was sharp, and mindful of his desire to ensure no hysterics were imminent, Christopher did as he was told. He turned carefully, his broad shoulders brushing against the door's sturdy frame, allowing himself to look at the woman in the bed fully for the first time. He couldn't tell how old she was, but her air of assurance, even when awoken from sleep by an intruder in her room, led him to believe she was no schoolroom miss. Of course, she wouldn't be. Sleeping here alone, she must be past an age when she would need a chaperone. From what he could make out, however, her looks didn't appear to be suffering from the effects of her advanced age. Black hair peeped out from a dainty lace cap and fell in silken coils around her modestly covered shoulders. Her skin in the golden light cast by the flickering blaze was pale, her high milky cheekbones standing out against the pale creaminess of the hollows below. Her full lips were sparkling jet in the dim light and though her eyes glittered he couldn't make out their color. He found himself hoping they were something unusual, something exotic to complement the unexpected contrast of dark hair and lucent skin.

"I locked my door when I came to bed. If you have truly made a mistake, how did you get into my room? If there is another key, please give it to me at once." There was a degree of command and self-possession in the whiskey-toned voice that, under the circumstances, Christopher couldn't help but admire. This was no milk and honey miss, no matter the pearly luster of her skin.

"I'm afraid the locks on these old mechanisms aren't all they should be. The innkeeper neglected to give me a key and so I assumed the door would be unlocked. I'm afraid that when it didn't instantly give way to my hand I used my shoulder to, er, persuade it." Christopher tried not to sound defensive, but he realized he was on shaky ground. "Again, please accept my apologies."

"What an odd thing to do," the woman said, thoughtfully. "I would rather have expected you to go down and see if you could find a key when the door refused to open."

It had been a great many years since Christopher had found himself blushing, but he did so now. How to explain to this remarkably self-possessed woman that his encounter with the busy fellow from across the hall had made him ill-inclined to slink back down the hallway? It sounded childish, even petulant.

"It's late and I didn't want to disturb anyone. It's quite dark downstairs." The explanation was sounding more and more foolish to his own ears. He couldn't imagine what it sounded like to hers. After another one of her long assessing looks, she seemed ready to dismiss the matter.

"I'm afraid you're going to have to steel yourself and confront the dark hallways nonetheless. I'll lock the door behind you," she said, continuing wryly after a short pause to let her words sink in. "Assuming the lock is capable of functioning, of course."

"I hadn't thought of that." Christopher looked around the room and spying a sturdy chair by the hearth, he picked it up and carried it over to the door. "This should serve as a bar to prevent anyone else getting in. Just put it under the catch to hold it in place after I've left."

"Thank you," the woman replied gravely. "I'm sure I'll manage."

"Well, goodbye then." Christopher inwardly groaned. He was acting like six kinds of fool and felt like a schoolboy. "Sleep well."

"Thank you," she repeated.

Somehow he managed to get out of the room without embarrassing himself any further, but it was a near thing. The door opened readily. Too readily. Closing it again took some dexterity. It was slightly off kilter, no doubt as a result of his earlier attempts to open it, and the latch showed a great deal of stubborn if inanimate reluctance to catch properly. As he wrestled with it, he heard soft movements from the other side. The woman he had disturbed was clearly waiting to bar the entrance once he had the door shut properly.

He finally managed with a bit of heavy lifting to line up the catch and the lever and was stepping away thankfully when he realized that in his hurry to escape the most awkward situation he had been in for some considerable time, he had left his travelling bag inside the room. He tapped gently on the door.

"Wait," he whispered. "I need to come back inside."

After a pause the door opened slowly and the woman's head peeped out.

"You cannot," she whispered harshly, her patience apparently at an end. "Go away or I'll scream."

Christopher tried to ignore the delightful vision she presented in her night rail and concentrate on the matter at hand. "I left my bag in your room. I can't go downstairs without it."

"Very well," she said somewhat crossly, opening the door fully. "Get it quickly, and for heaven's sake get out before someone sees you."

It was too late. The door across the hall opened and the inquisitive man who had earlier grilled Christopher once more peered out at him.

"Is there a problem, my lord?" he asked, now bristling with suspicion. "I'd be happy to call the landlord." He looked prepared to do just that, his earlier appeasement vanquished in the face of this new disturbance.

"No, thank you," Christopher replied at once. He moved away from the door, attempting to draw the fellow's eyes with him. But it was too late. Perhaps curiosity had slowed her reactions or her wits were still befuddled with sleep, but the woman did not withdraw into the room in time. Christopher's interrogator no sooner caught a glimpse of her than his expression changed completely.

"What's going on here?" he asked sharply. "This is a respectable house, I've been told. And up until now I've seen no reason to doubt it."

"You have no reason to doubt it now," Christopher replied, equally sharply, allowing the sharp edge of a tongue universally admired for its ability to cut pretension down to size to manifest. "This woman is…"

He got no further.

"Who is this man, my dear?" the woman asked, turning toward Christopher with a warning expression meant only for him.

"I have no idea," Christopher answered promptly. "But he seems dashed determined to interfere in my affairs."

"Well, come back to bed now. I'm sure the horses are fine and it wasn't colic causing that shivering."

The placid words had the desired effect on the man across the hall. Looking abashed, he muttered "I'm sorry, my lady. I didn't realize," and promptly shut the door.

"What are you doing?" Christopher asked in a scandalized whisper as she dragged him back through the door and closed it firmly.

"I have no wish to figure as some sort of doxy to be turned out into the night, sir," she said primly. "Or, I beg your pardon. It's 'my lord,' is it not?"

"What on earth has that to say to the matter?" Christopher demanded. "More to the point, if you don't wish your reputation to be ruined quite beyond repair, why did you drag a perfect stranger into your bedchamber?"

"You were well on your way to ruining my reputation without any help from me, my lord," she replied, anger deepening her voice and bringing out a hint of Irish roots. "You couldn't possibly have come up with an explanation for your presence in my room that would have satisfied that man. I don't know who he is and clearly you don't either. Let him go on thinking, therefore, that we are man and wife. We'll never see him again and no harm done."

"That's all very well," Christopher retorted, unwilling to consider that she might have a point. "But in the meantime, I'm stuck here in your bedroom!"

"Well, I'm very sorry, but I'll try not to take advantage of you."

Christopher could see that as soon as the words were spoken she regretted them. A deep crimson stained her cheeks and her hand came up to cover her mouth, presumably before any more unfortunate phrases could escape. Her eyes widened, and he saw for the first time that they were the deep blue of an evening's ocean with stars twinkling like sapphires in their luminous depths. He felt a twinge of satisfaction at the unexpectedness. He also noticed that she was younger than he had suspected when she seemed so eminently self-assured. In fact…he refused to allow his thoughts to travel any further. This was not the time.

Even if it most assuredly was the place.

Chapter Two

Caroline couldn't believe what she'd just said. If her uncle, her chaperone, her *maid*, anyone at all involved in her upbringing, had heard such a statement coming from her lips, she'd have been turned over a knee before the cat had time to lick its ear. She wished she could turn herself over her knee for allowing such a sentence to escape.

And if that wasn't bad enough, she could now clearly see for the first time what her intruder looked like.

Oh. My.

For one thing, he was several inches above the average height, just as she was. Though her height helped her horsemanship for that she was, of course, grateful, it did nothing for her comfort on the dance floor. She imagined being waltzed across the floor by someone who didn't need to reach up to clasp her waist. Someone she could look up to as they danced.

The jacket he wore, narrow across the waist, stretched across broad shoulders that would have no difficulty twirling her around. And his legs were definitely long enough to reach the ground. His hair, carelessly swept back from his brow, was as dark as her own. But his eyes were dark to match, and his complexion suggested someone who spent a good deal of time out of doors and didn't worry about the sun's rays.

He might be a peer of the realm, but she couldn't help thinking that he looked quite, quite peerless. She almost regretted her promise not to take advantage of him.

Thank heavens *that* thought hadn't been allowed to escape.

She took a deep breath and tried to pretend the last minute hadn't happened.

"In a few minutes he'll have gone back to sleep and you can retrieve your bag and go back downstairs. With a little luck we will neither of us see him in the morning. You can go on your way and I can go on mine."

She spoke as if it were the only possible solution, hoping the stranger would agree. After a long pause, he nodded.

"Yes, that seems to be the sensible, if unconventional way out of our dilemma. As long as we manage to avoid him for the remainder of our respective stays. It seems a little topsy turvy, but if we're to spend the next while together you must allow me to introduce myself. My name is Christopher Hawkins."

It suited him, Caroline thought. There was something hawk-like about his face and the way he focused so completely on her when he spoke.

"Not a lord?" She raised a brow.

"Well, yes, actually, I'm a viscount. My title is Lord Saxon."

Suddenly the muddle became clear.

"When I asked for a room earlier, they said there was one ready and were extremely deferential,"

Caroline exclaimed. "I thought it was some kind of English courtesy and dismissed it, but that explains what they meant—and why they were so very helpful."

She saw the look of polite puzzlement on his face and laughed. "My name is Caroline Saxon."

"Ah," A look of amusement and understanding relaxed the dark features. "So this is my room. And yours, too. They thought we were together."

"Clearly. Although why we should be arriving in separate rigs at completely different times seems to be something that didn't occur to them."

"It's not their place to question the comings and goings of the nobility," Christopher replied. Caroline's disapproval of such an arrogant sentiment only flashed quickly across her face before she schooled her features into immobility, but it didn't escape Christopher's notice. "I'm not suggesting they are correct in that judgement, just that it would not be worth their trouble to ask too many questions and risk losing a paying customer as long as things appear merely unusual rather than downright havey-cavey."

"But it does make the situation more difficult for us."

"Not really. I'll bed down in the parlour and quietly explain to Mr. Stafford in the morning."

"Now I know you have as much right to the room as I do, in fact, more since you booked it, I feel guilty sending you down to the dubious comforts of the salon. How will you manage?"

"I've slept in worse. At least it's dry, relatively warm and unlikely to be invaded by either hostile French soldiers or, worse, drunken Spanish allies. And no matter how miserable the night is, I'll have a hot meal to look forward to in the morning."

His words surprised Caroline. His cool elegance, despite his relative *dishabille*, had misled her into thinking him merely an ornament of society, if the word merely could fairly be used to describe a man she found so attractive. Yet his words suggested more than a passing familiarity with the recently concluded Spanish campaign. Had he fought with Wellington on the Peninsula? Clearly there was more to Lord Saxon than met the eye.

Now was hardly the time to find out.

"Practically Paradise in fact," Caroline mocked gently.

"Well, certainly not its opposite." The chestnut eyes darkened into an expression Caroline wasn't sure she understood. She was suddenly aware of her surroundings. The fire was burning well and its soft orange light served to emphasise the fact that it was the middle of the night and she was alone in a strange room with a strange man. She turned quickly to the bed and pulled off the soft patchwork coverlet, throwing it round her shoulders and hugging it tightly. Then, feeling foolish, she moved toward the fire as though her action had been one of mere physical discomfort, a sudden chill.

As if sensing her unease, Christopher kept as far from her as the small room allowed. "I can't risk running into our busy friend again, but I should be able to slip out in a few more minutes with no one the wiser." He crossed his arms in a deliberately casual manner and leaned against the small dressing table by the door. "So tell me about yourself, Miss Saxon. It is Miss, isn't it?"

"Yes, it is," she replied, grateful for the distraction. "I'm on my way to London from my home in Kerry. I'm to have 'a season' before I'll be allowed to return and get on with my life."

"But surely you can't be going to London on your own. I assume you have a respectable person with whom you will be staying, but where is your travelling companion?"

"I assure you, I'm well protected," Caroline said quickly. This was not the time to go into a long explanation about the coach accident that had injured her chaperone and forced her to continue on her own, especially to a chance-met stranger in a roadside inn. "I travel with my own coach and driver who take care of everything."

"A coach and driver! I hardly think that constitutes proper chaperonage." He sounded as censorious as a dowager duchess on a very high horse. "What was your family thinking to allow such a thing? Have you come all this way on your own?"

Caroline drew herself up to her full height and attempted to look down her nose at the impudence of his question. Even lounging across the room, however, he seemed to tower over her. "I hardly think that is any of your concern, my lord."

"It is the concern of anyone with sense and a modicum of decency. If you have travelled all this way on your own it's a miracle that some misfortune has not befallen you."

"Well, it has," Caroline shot back, annoyed at his highhanded belief that he had some sort of right to criticize her and her behavior. "That is why I find myself alone now. My carriage was overturned yesterday and my companion badly injured. I was forced to leave her in Cheston and continue on my own. Now, if that satisfies your unwarranted need to enquire into other people's affairs, perhaps you would be so good as to see whether the way is clear for you to depart."

"It's only been a couple of minutes. I don't dare risk it yet with the door so difficult to deal with," was the unfeeling response.

"Well, whose fault is that, barging into my room in the middle of the night?" Caroline knew she was being unfair, but it didn't stop her. The arrogance of the man!

"Entirely my own," Christopher replied, "for which I have already apologized, but I will do so again if it makes you feel better."

The humble response was unexpected. Caroline's gaze, which had been determinedly focussed on a point somewhere over his head, flew to his face in surprise. Although quick-tempered, Caroline was not one to hold a grudge and his readiness to admit fault disarmed her. As though he could see her capitulation, he smiled suddenly, an invitingly warm expression lightening his dark features. Her lips curled in response before she fully realized what she was doing.

"Tell me why you felt it incumbent to leave your companion behind. Surely if she was badly hurt it would have been logical to stay with her." His tone was mild, his deep rich voice seductive, and Caroline found herself more willing to impart information which she still considered none of his business.

"I have to reach London before the end of the month in order to fulfill the requirements of a legacy that was left me," she said, with some bitterness. "My companion was more incapacitated than hurt or I never would have left her, regardless of the legacy. She was on her way to meet a ship in England, The plan was for her to accompany me to London and then set off for Southampton. But if I had waited for her to accompany me, as she wanted me to, the delay would have meant she would miss the sailing. With me gone, she will be able to heal properly and still get there in time. It was only as a favor to my guardian that she agreed to accompany me in the first place. I couldn't let her suffer for it any more than she already was."

"I see," Christopher responded thoughtfully. "But why must you go to London for your legacy? Are there no lawyers in Ireland? If that's the case it sounds like heaven."

"Very amusing, my lord. Of course there are lawyers in Ireland. I imagine the entire world has been infested by the breed by now. It is not in order to visit a lawyer that I must go to London. My great aunt, who has recently died, left me twenty thousand pounds on condition that I have a season in London lasting no less than a full two months. I was on my way to fulfill her behest when the accident occurred."

"What an extraordinary condition." Christopher looked more amused than outraged. "Why would she stipulate such a thing?"

"Because, fond as I was of her, I believe she must have been all about in her head to suddenly start interfering in my life just because she took a dislike to…" Caroline suddenly realized that she was allowing herself to speak with inappropriate candor to one who was for all intents and purposes a complete stranger, even if he was in her bedroom in the middle of the night. How many more questions did he expect her to answer? His behavior was beyond inappropriate. She took a deep breath before continuing. "But that is neither here nor there. Surely enough time has passed so that it is safe for you to return downstairs," she concluded severely.

"I expect you are right," Christopher said, amusement and regret warring in the even tones of his voice. "While I'm determined to get to the bottom of why you consider your great aunt such a busybody and why and to whom or what she took such a dislike, it is very late. I daresay it can wait until morning."

He straightened up and walked toward the door as Caroline sputtered in indignation.

"I assure you, my lord, you will wait a good deal longer than that before your curiosity is assuaged. I fail to see how this can be considered any of your business."

"I'm afraid I have to agree with you," Christopher answered regretfully. "However, that is beside the case. I'm determined to discover the answers nonetheless."

"Well, you will not!"

Christopher held a finger up to his lips. "Shush, you'll wake our neighbour." He opened the door and carefully peered into the hallway before turning back to her. "The coast is clear. Don't forget to barricade the door."

Before Caroline could muster a response he had collected his bag and was gone, the door clicking shut gently behind him. A reluctant smile crossed her lips as she picked up the small chair to place under the inadequate locking mechanism. Nosy and highhanded though Lord Saxon may be, he was nevertheless also one of the most attractive men she had ever encountered.

Chapter Three

Despite the rigour of a day spent travelling alone and the unprecedented appearance of a strange man in her bedroom in the middle of the night, Caroline discovered early the next morning that she had been able to sleep surprisingly well. She woke up refreshed and feeling a degree of optimism about her situation that had been absent for some time—ever since she had first heard the terms of her great aunt's will, in fact.

She dressed quickly in a simple travelling outfit that was easy to fasten without the help of a maid, and spent as short a time as possible on her ablutions. She was eager to get on her way. Though how early she arrived in the city would make no difference in the overall scheme of things, she felt a readiness to begin fulfilling the terms of the will. For the first time she started to believe that her two months' residency in London would not stretch before her like eternity, every day and hour an ordeal to be endured and overcome before she could return to her home again; that there might be some previously unforeseen worth to her enforced sojourn beyond the financial gain that was critical to her future plans.

What she resolutely did not think, would not think, was that this new state of mind had anything to do with Lord Saxon.

When she got downstairs, she discovered that most

of the house's occupants remained firmly behind closed doors. She could hear a bustle from beyond the public area, but there seemed to be no one in either the salon or the taproom when she peeped inside. She was about to make her way down the passage toward where she assumed the kitchen lay when the front door opened and Lord Saxon stepped inside.

"Good lord," he said, startled. "You're an early riser."

"I'm not the only one, it would seem," Caroline answered, determined to be cordial.

"Well, I didn't have quite such a comfortable bed as I hope yours was," he replied as he carefully brushed off the shoulders of his jacket with lean, brown hands. "There's a bit of rain falling, but I believe it will clear before much longer. I don't think there has been enough to adversely affect the roads, so travelling should not present any problems. By the time you've had your breakfast, the weather should look much more amenable to continuing your journey with ease."

"Oh, that doesn't matter," she replied. "I shall manage no matter what the weather. Have you had the opportunity to speak to the proprietor about the mix-up with the room?"

"No, I've only seen the none-too-bright Bob and I fear any explanation of the situation would be beyond his limited grasp. However, I have sent him to round up some food, so if you'd care to join me, I'd be glad of your company."

"Thank you, my lord." Caroline's cautious tone caused a grin to cross Christopher's face. "Don't worry. I make it a firm rule never to ask intrusive questions over breakfast."

Caroline laughed. "In that case, I'd be glad to join you." As they entered the salon, the feeble light shining through the heavily mullioned window showed Christopher's face for the first time. His hair was slightly damp, and though his face looked clean enough, it was clear he had not yet shaved. It gave him a reckless air she found disturbing, and she spoke quickly.

"Do you not wish to tidy up beforehand?"

"Well, there's the rub," he answered, rubbing his bewhiskered chin. "I don't actually have anywhere to tidy up. I can hardly ask for hot water to be brought to the salon."

"You must use my room then. I'll go back up and ring for some more hot water. Come up in ten minutes and the room will be yours."

"That's very kind of you, but I don't think it's wise."

"Whyever not?" Caroline dismissed his qualms. "We've established that you have as much right to the room as I do. And as you said yourself, you really haven't spent a comfortable night. It's the least I can do. Perhaps it would be more proper for you to sit down to breakfast unshaven and uncomfortable, but it would be infinitely more sensible to do things my way."

An appreciative grin lightened Christopher's features. "Why can I not rid myself of the feeling that Miss Saxon's more sensible ways generally manage to be the paths most people find it incumbent upon themselves to follow?"

"Because most people are quite happy to do the sensible thing once it's been pointed out to them. It's just that most people have difficulty initially seeing the sensible path, unaccountable as that might be. I'm glad you're not one of them," she ended with a smile before tripping out the door and up the staircase to her...their room.

When Lord Saxon came downstairs twenty minutes later, Caroline had a hard time believing he could accomplish so much with the short amount of time allotted him. His dishevelment of the night before had been disturbingly attractive, and the rakish appearance he presented first thing in the morning had done things to her insides she was in no way prepared to acknowledge, even to herself. But with his cravat neatly tied, his hair smoothed into submission, and his clean-shaven face emphasizing the strong cheekbones beneath the rugged brown skin, he looked every inch the gentleman—and as dangerous as well-honed steel to a previously untouched heart.

Nonetheless, she spoke quite evenly, determined to maintain her customary calm. "There is coffee on the sideboard or ale, if you prefer. Shall I fetch some for you or would you rather serve yourself?"

"Thank you, but there's no need for you to wait on me. I'm quite capable of taking care of myself," Christopher replied, helping himself to a cup and saucer and pouring a long dark stream of coffee into it before sitting down at the small table across from her.

"Given the circumstances I thought it better to stay here in the private salon set aside for your use rather than venturing into the public rooms," Caroline said. "The fewer explanations we are forced to make the better, and I have no wish to participate in any conversations that would invariably lead to dissembling, if not outright deception."

"Sensible as always, Miss Saxon."

Caroline had always prided herself on that very quality. Yet somehow it didn't seem so estimable when acknowledged in such a way by such a man. While she didn't think he was laughing at her exactly, his dry tone and clipped words seemed so...lukewarm. She found herself foolishly wishing it were a less prosaic quality that elicited his approbation.

"Are you also on your way to London?" she asked, determinedly dismissing her uncharacteristic whimsy.

"Unfortunately, yes," he replied with a grimace. "I have been out of the country for some months and was making my leisurely way home when a family crisis erupted, and I was forced to hurry back and sort things out as best I could. Now, instead of returning to my estates as I'd hoped and intended, I have to waste more time going to town to assure my somewhat overprotective sister that her eldest son has been safely rescued from the brink of disaster. Judging from past experience, it will be some time before her nerves are back to normal."

His words sounded unwarrantedly callous to Caroline's ears, and she spoke without considering the fact that it was really none of her business. "Surely if her son was in danger she has every right to be concerned. I hardly think she can be accused of being overprotective in such a case."

"The only danger he faced was my temper, as well they both knew! I've been hauling the young rascal out of increasingly tiresome scraps since he was in short coats. Just once I'd like to see him manage to disentangle himself. My sister's only contribution has generally been a greater or lesser degree of weeping, depending on the seriousness of his latest start, and a fervently expressed appreciation of the fact that he has an uncle to deal with him. Well might she be thankful. She never lifts a finger herself to either repair the damage or see that he manages to keep out of trouble the next time one of his ill-considered antics gets the better of him." His frustration and annoyance were palpable. But Caroline heard an underlying note that mitigated both.

"How fortunate they are," Caroline said in some amusement, meeting his astonished look blandly. "I can see you are very fond of them both, my lord. It must be very comforting to them to know they have you to rely on."

Christopher narrowed his eyes at her suspiciously. "You don't have the temerity to be laughing at me, I hope."

"I wouldn't dream of it," she answered, the corner of her mouth only slightly curling upward. Her voice deepened as her words became more serious. "Indeed, I envy them. I would have loved to have had a brother I knew would have dropped everything to dash to the rescue of me and mine."

"Are you an only child then?"

"Yes, my mother died when I was born and my father not many years after. I don't remember her at all, of course, and I seldom saw him. They were both only children, so I was raised by a great aunt and uncle, but I used to dream of having a real family, someone to play with and to get into scrapes with, and someone to get me out of them again. It's very difficult to get into mischief if no one knows you're misbehaving. Either it passes for nothing, or you come to realize that you could very well have been badly hurt and no one the wiser, until it's too late for help to arrive." She paused for a moment before continuing briskly. "However, I dare say it wouldn't have suited me at all to have a parent telling me what to do and interfering with my pursuits, not to mention having siblings constantly competing for attention and expecting me to share."

If Christopher thought her words inadvertently revealed a childhood that sounded more than a little lonely he was too wise to say so. Pity was not an emotion likely to inspire gratitude in the formidable Miss Saxon.

"I'm sure there are many who would envy you your freedom," he contented himself with saying.

"Yes, I'm sure you're right."

Before she could say more, the door opened and Bob came in with a platter laden with food. He grinned at them good-naturedly as he carefully balanced the tray on the sideboard and began unloading the dishes.

"I'll just pop these down here and leave you to sort yourselves out," he said. "Right busy we are, so I don't have time to wait on table. Happen that's best, anyway. Too much bustle at breakfast makes for no peace the entire day, my old dad used to say."

"That will be fine," Caroline said quickly, the outraged gleam in Christopher's eye causing her to step in before he put the hapless servant firmly in his place. "We can certainly manage on our own." She rose and surveyed the dishes laid out before her. "This looks lovely. We'll certainly be able to continue on our way without worrying about provisions. Thank you very much."

Bob beamed at her and nodded his head several

times in his enthusiasm as he backed toward the door.

"Just a minute, er, Bob," Christopher commanded. "Please ask Mr. Stafford to come in when he has a minute to spare. I wish to speak to him."

Looking somewhat nervous, Bob agreed he'd send the boss in right sharp and hurriedly exited.

"You've frightened him," Caroline scolded as she helped herself to a plate and began to pile it with ham and an assortment from the accompanying dishes. "Now he's going to think he's done something wrong and you mean to complain to the proprietor."

"Well, that was certainly not my intention. However, perhaps if he were more attentive he wouldn't have allowed one room to be allotted to two different people. Let it be a lesson to him."

"You're not going to say that to Mr. Stafford, I hope," Caroline exclaimed. "You could lose the poor man his position and I'm sure there aren't so many jobs available in such an out-of-the-way place as this that he could easily find another one."

"I'm quite convinced he would have a great deal of difficulty finding another one under any circumstances," Christopher replied grimly. "I can't imagine how he managed to snabble this one. The man's a complete fool. However, I merely wanted to warn our host of our somewhat unorthodox arrangement and ensure there are no awkward questions asked."

"Well, please be careful how you phrase it. The poor man doesn't deserve to be turned off."

"My dear Miss Saxon, I have no intention of making the life of some half-witted rustic any worse than it already is, so please acquit me of the desire to persecute him. I will simply explain the situation in which we find ourselves and leave Bob to the devil, who will no doubt be nowhere near as pleased to receive him as I will be to see the last of him."

Picking up a plate, he marched determinedly to the sideboard and began to help himself to a stack of beef that would have fed both himself and several hungry contemporaries. Caroline merely smiled and applied herself to her more modest repast. By the time they had eaten their fill, the contents of both plates were considerably reduced and both tempers were considerably restored. Christopher pushed his plate away and sat back, viewing his companion speculatively.

"I still cannot like the idea of you traveling completely unaccompanied," he said. "I believe it behooves me to escort you the rest of your way." He held up his hand to forestall the protest he could clearly see forming. "We are both travelling to London, so it is hardly an inconvenience, and it would certainly set my mind at rest."

Caroline was not so ready to fall in with his wishes.

"I assure you there is not the slightest necessity. I have come this far and I am quite capable of travelling the rest of the way."

"I daresay that's true," was the mild response. "But I would be a nervous wreck by the time I arrived in town, which would severely inhibit my ability to calm my sister down. So I beg you to do what I ask for my sake and for hers if you won't do it for yourself. I won't say you owe it to me, of course, for letting you have my room, since I couldn't possibly have slept a wink in my warm, comfortable bed knowing you were downstairs tossing and turning all night in a vain attempt to snatch just a few moments of rest."

Caroline laughed, a low throaty chuckle that lit her face like a sunbeam. "Clearly after the night you've been put through it would hardly be right to cause you any more distress. Very well, you may escort me to London."

"Thank you. My mind is already easier. Now, breakfast is concluded and my promise no longer stands. Tell me why you are obliged to travel to the city in order to receive your inheritance."

"My lord!" Caroline was taken aback by the question. "I have agreed to your escort. I have not agreed to your interference in my affairs. It can be no possible business of yours why I must go to London."

"Humor me, Miss Saxon. I mean to find out, and I'm devilishly obstinate when it comes to getting my own way."

Looking at his carelessly laughing face, Caroline had no difficulty in believing that he was generally able to convince anyone to accede to his demands. And suddenly her reticence seemed foolish.

"Very well," she said. "I can see I'll have no peace until you've made my business your own."

"Very wise," was the prompt reply. "Now spill your budget." He poured himself another cup of coffee and sat back with the air of a man willing to take however long necessary to hear the entire tale.

"Well," Caroline began. "I told you I was raised by my great aunt and great uncle. They were brother and sister who never married and kept house together in Kerry. When my parents died they decided to take me in, since they were beyond the age when it was likely that they would ever marry and have children of their own, and their brief experience of my earlier visits when my father left me with them made them decide that not only would they enjoy an experience they had previously considered beyond their grasp, but they would then have someone to care for them in their old age. And, really, when it came right down to it, there was no one else to take me. They couldn't have a Saxon thrown on the parish."

Though she sounded quite cheerful, the apprehension she had felt as a small child destined to live with two elderly people set in their ways and with no real experience of dealing with children came through. She was completely unconscious of the fact that her hands were knotted in her lap or that she was speaking more quickly than she was accustomed to doing. Her eyes were fixed on a point beyond Christopher's shoulder as though she were seeing that child in her mind's eye as, clothed all in black, she stepped out of the carriage that had delivered her to her new life.

"It must have been very lonely," Christopher remarked gently.

She brought her attention back to him abruptly and shook her head. "On the contrary, we dealt very well together. I took care not to interfere too much with their established habits and customs, and they allowed me to go my own way. I grew up doing as I pleased with a degree of freedom I fancy most children only dream of. I had an entire library to educate myself with and all the outdoors at my doorstep to run as wild in as I wished."

"And did you run wild?"

"Indeed! I soon discovered some of the children

whose parents worked about the estate and I led them on many an adventure. I believe if my aunt and uncle had discovered half the trouble into which I was constantly embroiling myself they would both have dropped into an apoplectic fit on the spot."

"You seem like a remarkably civilized young woman to be the product of such a harum-scarum upbringing," Christopher observed as he helped himself to another cup of coffee and poured one for Caroline. "Were you eventually put into the care of a nurse or governess?"

"Oh, no," Caroline laughed, accepting the steaming cup gratefully and taking a long swallow before continuing. "I don't believe it would have occurred to either one of them that I needed such a thing. My guardians were somewhat eccentric. My great uncle lives for his genealogical research, you see, and my great aunt was a champion botanist. As I grew older, I came to realize that they needed my help every bit as much as I needed theirs. So I allowed myself to be tamed by the housekeeper, who had long disapproved of my wild ways and was quite happy to wrestle me into some semblance of a civilized being. When the time was right, I took over the running of the household and it worked out very well. My aunt and uncle were able to devote themselves to their studies in considerably more comfort than they had managed in the past, and my penchant for bossiness was given a more constructive outlet than leading the local children into trouble on a daily basis. Besides, their parents were starting to complain," she concluded with what looked suspiciously like a grin.

"It must have seemed very dull after previously

being allowed so much freedom."

"I suppose so, but I was very glad to be useful and busy about something. I don't like to be idle, you know."

"I can well imagine," Christopher retorted. "You seem most redoubtable to me, and I'm sure that if you set your mind to running a household it would soon become a model of efficiency whether you had any previous experience or not. But something tells me your efforts weren't met with unqualified approbation. Did your aunt and uncle resent your management of their domestic affairs?"

"Oh, no, not at first. I don't believe my uncle noticed and my aunt was glad to have the running of the household handled by someone else. She had never been very good at it, since her interests lay elsewhere."

"So what put the fly in the ointment of the efficiently run life of the practical Miss Saxon?"

Caroline's expression darkened, the humor that had been so apparent as she spoke of running wild with the other children disappearing like fog off sun-heated hills.

"Well, my aunt suddenly took it into her head that I had been left too much alone and was on my way to being as reclusive as she was herself, although why she thought that was a problem is anyone's guess, since it was the life she chose for herself. She received a letter from an old friend that reminded her of her younger days and it made her realize I had never been out in society much, simply because they had always routinely refused most invitations and people in the county around eventually stopped asking them. She quite unreasonably decided that I, too, should have the opportunity to go to London and make my curtsy to society. It was quite ridiculous and I believed I had convinced her to put it out of her mind."

"Yet here you are on your way."

"Yes, unfortunately. She quite took me by surprise. My great uncle's estate is entailed on a second cousin. I have always known this, and also that the money promised me by my aunt would be enough to keep me comfortable, as well as enable me to pursue an ambition I have been dreaming of for several years. I can't think how she came to get such a bee in her bonnet and overset my plans so completely, but she did. When she died quite suddenly of a lung ailment from tending her plants through an ice storm, I discovered that she had recently rewritten her will. The money I had been counting on will only come into my possession if I do as she had commanded and present myself for a London season."

Christopher sat up rather abruptly from the lounging position he had maintained while listening to Caroline's story. "Are you saying your aunt was willing to allow you to become both penniless and homeless if you didn't fulfill her conditions? That seems very harsh from someone who I assume has stood in the place of a mother to you for all your life." Though he was clearly trying not to sound judgemental, the stormy tilt of his eyebrows and the harsh tones of his voice plainly conveyed his disapprobation of such a manoeuvre. His hand clenched on the handle of his cup, making his fingernails white against the sun-roughened skin of his hands. "Excuse me if my question upsets you, but could she have been of sound mind when she made such a stipulation, knowing that she could place you in the most precarious of circumstances?"

"I'm afraid that much as I may wish to, I cannot accuse her of being mad," Caroline answered prosaically enough. "On the contrary, what she did was very cunning. She knew she could rely on my practical nature to accede to her demands, rather than fly off the handle and call the world well lost for love or some other nonsense in a fit of pique."

Christopher sat back, a look of amusement on his face. "Ah, so now we get to the crux of the matter. There's a love interest, and if I draw the correct conclusions from something you let slip last night, it's not a connection your great aunt approves of."

Caroline drew herself up from the casual, confiding pose she had assumed while telling her story, elbows on the table and small, rounded chin resting in her clasped hands. "I believe I've explained enough to assuage your curiosity, my lord," she said with gentle dignity, her chin high and her back straight against the rungs of her chair. "I hardly need go into every detail. Suffice it to say, my aunt did not approve of all my plans and hit upon this method to put an end to them. While I have no choice but to go along with her wishes to a certain extent, she cannot prevent me putting the money to any use I choose once I have fulfilled the will's requirements and it truly becomes my money."

"So what do you mean to do with it?" Christopher persisted.

Caroline paused a moment before answering, but she realized the questions was fair enough and so confessed, "I mean to start a horse breeding center. Ireland's horses are justifiably acclaimed as the best in the world. But all too often it's the result of luck as much as anything else. I believe that if the subject were approached scientifically we would be able to breed horses to exhibit very specific qualities, not just grays or bays, but horses that run faster or have a calmer temperament. To my mind there's no limit to what could be accomplished, but it must be done logically, not in the haphazard manner that now prevails." As she spoke her enthusiasm for the subject became more and more apparent, the honeyed inflection in her voice rising and a pink hue coming to the alabaster cheeks.

"But surely blood lines have always been important in horse breeding. It's impossible to go to Tattersall's without being regaled with the parentage of some animal or another someone's trying to sell. Since *Weatherby's Stud Book* came out, breeding lines seem to be all anyone talks about anymore. I don't see what you would do that would be so very different." Christopher tried to keep the doubt out of his voice, but he clearly considered the scheme an impractical one.

"I assure you I have thought it through and there's no reason to believe it wouldn't be quite workable." Caroline's withdrawal was as apparent as her earlier enthusiasm had been. "The very fact that people are interested in Mr. Weatherby's book shows there is a market for animals that have been bred in a truly scientific manner. Besides, he only deals with thoroughbreds for racing. I mean to expand the concept to riding horses, someday perhaps even carriage horses. My animals will be certified and guaranteed to be as perfect as the well-thought-out mixing of the required strains can accomplish. It won't simply be a matter of my fast goer mating with your fast goer, but of…" She broke off abruptly. "Oh, what's the use. I couldn't get my aunt to believe me, and she spent her life developing new strains of plants in exactly the way I mean to with horses. I couldn't expect you to understand."

"I am sure your aunt, just like me, was only concerned that you not get swept away by enthusiasm for a scheme that may have little chance of success," Christopher replied, stung.

"That's all very well," was Caroline's quick response. "But what neither of you is taking into consideration is the fact that I have considered all this very carefully, and am quite able to form a rational plan without the interference of those who feel they know better than me just because of their age or station in life or sex." She paused, raking him with a searing flick of her eyes before continuing, "My lord."

She rose from the table, and nose held high, moved toward the door. "Now, if you will excuse me, I wish to collect my things together so we can be on our way."

"I have noticed, Miss Saxon..." Christopher began when the sound of raised voices penetrated from the passageway. His eyes narrowed suddenly, and whatever he had been about to say was forestalled as, raising a peremptory hand in a demand for immediate silence, he listened to the ruckus beyond the door. A rueful expression crossed his features and he just had time to say, "I believe the fat is in the fire," before the door burst open.

A petite blonde dressed in the very latest and most dashing mode swept into the room without sparing a glance for the horrified Mr. Stafford who followed her, his hands wringing in consternation as he attempted to stop her precipitous entry. "Madam, I beg you. That is a private room," he cried in vain. "I cannot allow you to enter."

"Nonsense," was the dismissive response. "Lord Saxon and I are old friends. He would certainly be cross were he to discover we had shared the same inn and he hadn't known." She moved determinedly toward her quarry, hands beautifully clad in the finest kid glove extended, full red lips stretched wide in a glittering smile.

"Christopher, how pleased I am to see you back in England again. We've been expecting you any time this age and wondering what could have become of you."

With little choice in the face of such a determined assault, Christopher took her hands in his own and raised one to his lips.

"Annabelle," he said, the weariness in his voice discernible to only the most sensitive of listeners. "I've only just returned. Except for Eleanor and the cub, no one knows I'm back yet. At least, no one knew until now. What a surprise to run into you so soon after my return. What are you doing here?"

"Oh, my sister and her husband are taking me to visit their home in Berkshire and we stopped here last night. Perhaps you know that my sister Clarissa recently married. Or perhaps you don't know. You've been so very out of touch this last little while." She gave a merry little tinkle of a laugh. "In any event it was my brother-in-law who told me that he ran into you last night in the most dubious of circumstances. He only mentioned it because he knew you were a particular friend of mine. But the absurd creature got it completely wrong. He told me you were staying here with your wife. Of course, I assured him he was mistaken." She took a step closer and looked up into his eyes, a trembling smile hovering on her lips. "No one knows better than I that such a thing couldn't possibly be true."

Her winsome expression seemed to be wasted on its object. Lord Saxon stepped back and answered coolly. "On the contrary, Annabelle. Your brother-in-law did have the honor of...well, meeting would perhaps be too strong a word. Let us say, encountering my wife last night. Allow me to introduce you."

Ignoring the indignant gasp he had no hesitation in attributing to his newly claimed bride, he turned his back on the petite blonde beauty and crossed the room to where Caroline had been standing in the shadow of the wide flung door. His eyes narrowed in warning and, unable to think of any way out of the mess into which they were rapidly becoming entangled, Caroline saw no choice but to go along with the charade in hopes of somehow coming out of it with a modicum of dignity. For her reputation she was considerably less optimistic. Ruin seemed inevitable. But concluding that a scandal deferred was preferable to a scandal imminent, she held out her hand and allowed him to tuck it under his arm and draw her forward into the centre of the room.

"My dear, allow me to present Miss Annabelle Winthrop. Annabelle, this is my wife, Caroline, Lady Saxon."

"How do you do," Caroline said politely, holding out her right hand and surreptitiously pulling the other one deeper into the crook of Christopher's arm so the lack of a wedding ring on her finger would not be noticeable.

"How do you do," the woman replied, a puzzled look creasing her carefully arched brow. "You must excuse me if I seem a little taken aback. I had no idea Christopher was contemplating such a change in his situation. At least not…" she halted abruptly and turned toward him. "I…you should have let us know," she said simply.

"I'm afraid it was something of a whirlwind romance. I barely knew myself from one minute to the next what was happening. We were quite, er, swept away by circumstances."

"My lord," Caroline said with a warning look. "You mustn't give Miss Winthrop the wrong idea."

"Oh, no!" That lady interjected hastily and with obvious mendacity. "I quite understand. I'm so sorry I barged in on you like that. You must be wishing me at Jericho and in any case my sister will be wondering what's become of me. I must be on my way. Perhaps we'll see you in London when I return. It was lovely to meet you, Lady Saxon." She gave the couple a small, tight smile and quickly made her escape.

No sooner had she left the room than Caroline rounded on her ersatz husband. "My lord! What can you have been thinking?" It was clear she was wound up to deliver a scathing rebuke, but she had only begun when a small sound behind her recalled to her mind the presence of the inn's proprietor. It soon became clear that his indignation was equal to her own.

"My lord!" Mr. Stafford cried, unconsciously echoing Caroline's words. "This is a respectable establishment. Never have we witnessed such an outrage. I take leave to tell you this kind of behavior is not what we are used to here, indeed it is not!"

"So I should hope," Christopher interjected before the beleaguered man had a chance to continue.

"Apparently my wife and I were mistaken in our assumption that we would be granted a modicum of privacy when we've paid down good money for a private salon. I presume you have an explanation for why other guests are allowed to wander into our room at their pleasure with no one to say them nay."

Mr. Stafford looked appalled. "That's not what I meant!"

Christopher looked down his nose and it was as if ten generations of Saxons stood behind him, ready as one to put the poor man permanently in his place with a single concerted show of disdain. "I fail to see what else you could possibly mean."

But Mr. Stafford was made of sterner stuff than his demeanor showed and he was not prepared to back down in the face of ever so many generations of righteous privilege. He carried on gamely. "I mean…this…lady, my lord. You said nothing about her when you booked in. Indeed…"

"Aha!" Christopher allowed a look of understanding to pass over his features. "I see your error. My wife knew I'd be stopping the night here and drove over to meet me. It was as much a surprise to me as it is to you, although a delightful one." He turned toward Caroline and raised her hand to his lips in a way that brought a blush of confusion to her cheeks and unaccountably reassured the harassed innkeeper, before turning back. "That, of course, explains the confusion in the register last night. My wife arrived before me, and naturally, was shown to my room."

The innkeeper knew when he was beaten, whatever the truth of the situation. Backing down with as much dignity as he could muster, he bowed to the man and woman standing so united before him. "Of course, my lord. My lady. Forgive me. And forgive me also for the intrusion. I had no idea the young lady would burst in when she had been told this was a private salon."

Lord Saxon was prepared to be gracious. "Yes, well, Miss Winthrop has always been impulsive. I doubt you could do much to restrain her."

Mr. Stafford's relief was as great as his indignation had been. After hearing they were ready to depart, he assured the pair he would have their bill ready in jig time and bowed himself out of the room, calling as soon as he was past the threshold for the hapless Bob.

"My lord," Caroline began again, when she could be reasonably certain of not being overheard. "What on earth are you about?"

"I told you the fat was in the fire. There was no other way to prevent the deuce of a scandal and I have no wish to figure as the vile seducer of some poor country girl who fell so ripely into my clutches."

Caroline was not reassured and had no hesitation in showing it. "That's all very well. I have no wish to figure as a fool of a country girl ready to fall into your clutches. But I fail to see how this deception is going to help."

"It isn't, in and of itself," he said with a grim note in his voice. "But when society sees that we are well and truly married, the issue will simply not arise."

Chapter Four

Caroline couldn't believe what she was hearing.

"Have you lost your mind? I can't marry you. I don't even know you. We only met for the first time last night!"

"Shhh! You'll bring the whole scheme down around our heads and then we really will be forced to marry."

"But…" Caroline paused and took a deep breath. This was clearly no time for hysterics even if her nerves would have welcomed the release. "Are you saying you have a plan that will disentangle us from this mess?" she asked in a more moderate tone.

Christopher's mouth turned up in a smile of approval. "Redoubtable Miss Saxon. I knew it wouldn't take long for you to come back to your sensible self. If you will trust me for a little while longer, I suggest we collect our bags and head out as quickly as possible. I will explain my idea on the way to London. We'll be able to talk without interruption, with no one the wiser to the topic of our conversation, and I have every faith in my ability to persuade you to my way of thinking."

"I had not thought to ride with you in your carriage. My coachman will not approve."

"He'll approve even less when he sees I'm tooling my own curricle, but it can't be helped. We must talk, and I feel sure you will manage to overcome his misgivings. I suggest you get right to it before some busybody takes it upon themselves to inform him that you have acquired a husband during the night."

"Good God! I completely forgot about that aspect of the situation. Thank heavens my maid stayed behind to tend to my companion. I'll go and speak to him right away and then pack my bags."

She hurried out of the room and made her way briskly down the passage toward the back door that led to the stables. Meanwhile, Christopher, who was not so sanguine about Mr. Stafford's continued compliance, sought out the proprietor, and with a few judicious words and a more substantial addition to the reckoning than he was used to paying, managed to persuade him that any gossip about Lord Saxon and his surprise bride would be a serious mistake.

It wasn't much above half an hour later that Caroline was being helped into his lordship's carriage as her bags were somewhat precariously tied to the sporty vehicle's back.

"I must proffer my apologies," Christopher remarked. "I didn't expect to have to convey the better part of the entire inventory of the Irish millinery trade."

Caroline smiled down at him as she carefully arranged the folds of a royal blue travelling rug around her knees. "No, indeed. It's certainly a good thing I decided to take advantage of my enforced residence in London to supplement my wardrobe. Had I brought everything I'm told would be necessary for a successful season there would never have been enough room for all my trunks," she said primly.

A reluctant grin passed his lips. "Are you ever at a loss for words, Miss Saxon?" he asked as he climbed up beside her and took up the reins.

"I believe I have an adequate vocabulary for my needs," she said, as Christopher easily guided the horses out of the inn's yard and onto the highway.

"You certainly had the words to persuade your coachman to leave you to my tender mercies. I can't help but be curious about how you managed that feat."

Caroline folded her hands primly in her lap and glanced up at him. "You can't help but be curious about a lot of things that aren't really your concern, can you, my lord?"

"True, Miss Saxon. It's considered one of my more serious failings. I'm afraid the only cure is to have my curiosity satisfied."

"Well, since the problem is clearly a recurring one, that sounds like a temporary cure at best. However, I'm sure you won't die of the disease, so you may as well get used to living with it," was the heartless reply. "Now, perhaps you would be good enough to explain to me how we're to get out of this wretched fix."

"And in exchange you can tell me how you fobbed your coachman off."

Caroline's frown was rendered unconvincing by the upward tilt at the corner of her mouth she couldn't quite manage to get under control. A small dimple peeped becomingly and Christopher grinned at the sight, causing her to sigh and roll her eyes in an exaggerated manner. "Very well, my lord. I suppose such tenacity should be rewarded even if your audacity should not. But you must first convince me that your solution is truly workable."

There was a short pause and while Christopher was too good a whip to fiddle with the reins it was clear he was uneasy. His voice was uncharacteristically grave as he spoke.

"Miss Saxon, to be frank, I believe we are in quite a coil. We might have pulled it off if that wretched chit hadn't burst in on us, but the fat is truly in the fire now. I've scoured my brain for a solution, and while my plan is both radical and convoluted, it is the only one I can come up with that gets us off without involving either a dreadful scandal or an actual marriage. And while I appreciate your manifold charms, and am quite convinced there are many more to uncover, I'm not quite ready yet to become leg-shackled to a chance-met stranger, no matter how beguiling, if there is some way to avoid it. Do you agree?"

Caroline savoured the somewhat startling idea that she could be described as beguiling. Compliments, even if they could be attributed to good breeding and an easy manner rather than sincerity, did not come her way very often. And was she really in possession of manifold charms? Regretfully, she had to dismiss his absurd words—such flummery must come as natural as breathing to a man of such easy manner, and it made her own voice sharper as she replied. "Certainly I agree! I have no intention of marrying a man about whom almost the only thing I know is his propensity for sneaking into other people's rooms."

"It's kind of you to call it sneaking when I had to burst the lock to do so. And to be fair, you also know I'm equally talented at sneaking out of them again," was the meek reply.

"That is not a virtue, my lord!"

"No, I don't suppose the practical Miss Saxon would consider that a virtue. Although in certain circles it could come in decidedly handy."

His words were deliberately provocative and Caroline refused to rise to the bait, saying merely "I don't doubt it. Fortunately, they are not circles I have the slightest intention of becoming in any degree acquainted with. Now, if we may return to the matter at hand, what is your plan?"

"Answer me a question first, Miss Saxon." He held up a hand to forestall her inevitable protest. "I assure you the answer is critical to the operation of my plan." When he saw that she had pressed her lips firmly together he continued, "Are you absolutely determined to go ahead with this Irish horse farm as soon as you've fulfilled the terms of your aunt's bequest?"

"I've already told you so."

"And you have no intention of returning to London and seeking a place in society?"

"None whatsoever," was the disdainful reply.

"And no one in London knows you except for this friend of your late aunt?"

"She doesn't know me because we've never met," Caroline answered with an inborn commitment to the absolute truth. "But she is certainly my only connection in the city. Why?"

"In order for my plan to work it's crucial that you never appear in society again after the two-month term of your aunt's condition is fulfilled. Are you sure that's acceptable to you?"

"I have no interest in becoming a frivolous society creature, I assure you." She lifted her shoulder in rejection of the very notion. "Once I've done what I have been compelled to do, I'll be quite content to return to my home and never see London again. I will secure an agent to oversee that side of my business."

"Then, Miss Saxon, for the next two months you are going to dispense with the Miss and become, for all intents and purposes, Lady Saxon instead."

"And this will somehow save my reputation?" Caroline allowed the incredulousness she was feeling to show. "I wish you might explain yourself, but I fail to see how you will be able to do so."

If he had expected either swooning or a sharp slap Christopher was doomed to disappointment. He cast an admiring glance in her direction. Her eyes were fixed steadily on the road before them and if she felt any trace of embarrassment it wasn't apparent in the smooth angle of the ivory cheek that presented itself to him under her chip straw bonnet. Miss Saxon might be many things, but tiresomely emotional was not one of them. He wondered if she would ever be capable of throwing a tantrum or making a scene and was devoutly glad to consider it extremely unlikely. It would make his rather startling plan that much easier to both broach and carry out.

"I have been out of England for the better part of a year and had barely managed to unpack a valise when that tiresome nephew of mine started kicking over the traces. My servants hardly had time to realize I was home before I set off again, never mind anyone else. In other words, the news of my return to England shouldn't have spread outside my home. I had planned to continue on to my estate in Dorset after dealing with Michael and reassuring my sister in London. However, I think that plan must be delayed. It's time for me to arrive in London as if for the first time since I returned from abroad. I shall make my bow to society and you,

Miss Saxon, shall make yours at my side, having been swept off your feet and onto English soil before your good sense had a chance to overcome your shockingly underdeveloped, but clearly rebellious, sensibility."

He risked a glance in her direction to see her reaction so far. No appearance of outrage or indignation. So far so good. "We will play the honeymoon couple so convincingly that no one will be the wiser, and while you will, of necessity, be obliged to stay at my townhouse I assure you your virtue will remain as unblemished as it is now. At the end of two months, during which we will convince the *ton* that we are the happiest of newly married couples, I will take you off to visit 'our' estate. Soon after a tragic accident will befall you. Lady Saxon will be no more and her grief-stricken husband will, in the fullness of time, return to London alone. Meanwhile, you will be free to return to your rustic paradise and breed horses to your heart's content. As long as you stay in Ireland, there should be virtually no chance of our deception being discovered."

When he finished speaking Caroline didn't immediately respond. Christopher wasn't sure if that was a good sign or not. He wasn't even sure what a good sign would indicate. The prospect before them was wearisome, time-consuming, and he admitted to himself, damned inconvenient. They would spend months on edge, forced into each other's company, with their own plans on hold, just because of a foolish mistake on the part of an innkeeper's half-witted assistant. It seemed a high price to pay for stumbling through the wrong door—especially since he'd played the part of a perfect gentleman and left again as soon as he safely could!

Once more he shot her a glance to try to gauge her reaction. Her lower lip jutted out and there was a slight frown wrinkling the fine arch at the top of her nose. Her eyes seemed to be focused somewhere between the upright black ears of his leader. She was clearly thinking hard and a swell of admiration coursed through him. Miss Saxon was indeed something rare, a woman who had the courage to play with the cards she was dealt, and the intelligence to think about how to do so to the best advantage. She neither complained about her lot nor relied on someone else to get her out of trouble. Clearly she would go along with his plan only if and when she herself deemed it to be a good one.

"We would have scraped through nicely if not for that unfortunate meeting with Miss Winthrop this morning," she said, her musing tone of voice clearly indicating that she was as yet unconvinced. "Your plan seems unnecessarily convoluted. Is there no possibility of taking the young lady into our confidence and convincing her to remain quiet about our encounter? Surely she can be made to understand the impossible position we have been put in through no fault of our own."

"You'd have as much success persuading a cat to spit out a salmon," was the blunt reply. "Oh, I don't doubt she'd mean to keep it quiet, but before long she'd simply 'have' to confide in her closest friend and then in another one, and before the cat had time to lick its ear, everyone from the highest-ranking duchess to the lowliest milliner's apprentice would be in on the secret. And I assure you, there are very few members of 'the best society' who wouldn't be completely titillated and thoroughly convinced there was a great deal more to the story. It would become the *on dit* of the season. You would be ruined and I would be branded as something much less than a gentleman in no short order."

"Well, we can't have that," Caroline responded immediately, much to Christopher's relief. "It seems a remarkably cumbersome plan, however. Is there not a simpler solution than spending months forced together in such a charade?"

"If you can come up with one, I'll be more than happy to follow your dictates." In an attempt to alleviate his own qualms as much as reassure his companion he continued. "It will quite probably work out to be not as bad as it sounds at first. You're committed to staying in London for the designated period of time—you'll just be doing it in different circumstances than you had originally envisioned. I have been away and have no commitments at the current time, so my plans won't need to be reorganized to any great degree."

"Clearly," Caroline said, with an almost mischievous grin tipping up the corner of her shapely mouth, "nothing could be easier. In fact, if one were determined to embroil oneself in such a coil one would be shockingly remiss not to take advantage of this opportunity."

"Quite so," Christopher agreed solemnly. "The only thing we must clarify is the exact wording of your aunt's will. Did she make any stipulations about how you were to spend your time in London? If so, we may be at a standstill before we start."

Caroline looked startled. "I don't know. The lawyer read the will and explained in the most general terms.

He made all the arrangements for my trip and I just went along with it. Whether or not there were specific instructions beyond the time I was to spend there I have no idea."

"I'll consult my own lawyer when we get to town. He should be able to uncover the details."

"Is that wise? You'll surely be forced to take him into your confidence if you do so."

"I'll need to in any case. I can hardly come prancing into London with a brand-new bride in tow and *not* consult my lawyer. It would be one of my first priorities were we really married. As for taking him into my confidence, his firm has served as my family's solicitors for years. If he can't be trusted to keep my affairs in the strictest confidence, then no one can."

"I don't know whether to hope he can find no flaw in your scheme, or wish for the opposite," Caroline said in some vexation. "My lord, I feel like over the last few weeks I've been repeatedly turned head over heels and have no say in the matter of my future at all. It's not a little disconcerting."

"Yes, I can tell by the way you've suddenly taken to calling me 'my lord' again." He paused briefly before continuing. "Miss Saxon, I fully recognise that you have been placed in an untenable position. All I can do is assure you that it is not one I will take advantage of. We will attempt to get over the ground as lightly as possible and while there may be obstacles ahead, I have every confidence we will manage."

"Thank you, my lo…Christopher," she said. Though he didn't take his eye off his horses or his hands off the reins, Caroline had a sudden sense of being clasped in comfort. It was an unusual feeling for one who, through no fault of her own, had been forced to cultivate independence from an early age. She changed the subject abruptly. "These are certainly prime goers," she said brightly. "We must be making good time. When do you expect us to arrive in London?"

"Since you're planning to go into the horseflesh business a compliment from you is praise indeed. In fact, we shouldn't be too long on the road at all. Another hour or so should see us within sight of the city."

With his words Caroline realized that without her noticing, traffic had indeed been picking up. Christopher was forced to pay more attention to his driving and she was content to sit back and allow herself a few minutes of calm in the midst of the storm that seemed to have recently wracked her existence. The way her world continued to spin, she certainly couldn't look forward to many in the future.

Chapter Five

By the time Christopher stopped the curricle in front of a pink stuccoed townhouse in Berkeley Square, Caroline felt as if every sense had been assailed. The sounds, the smells, the sights of the capital were overwhelming to one raised on the outskirts of a very small village far from the bustle of city life. Her journey across England had opened her eyes to a certain extent, but London was in a class by itself. With some relief she noticed the plane trees that graced the center of the square. Their mottled bark and green canopy looked like a small piece of Ireland set down in the midst of an alien land.

Christopher had barely helped her down when the front door of the townhouse burst open and a woman catapulted outside.

"Christopher, at last!" she cried as, clutching the skirts of a dashing blue dress, she flew down the steps to throw herself into his arms. After a quick hug she grasped hold of his sleeves in a firm grip and pelted him with questions, shaking his arms for emphasis with every question. "Is everything all right? Did you stop them? Is Michael safe from that...?" Words seemed to fail her and she looked up into his eyes beseechingly.

"Michael is fine, far better than he has any right to be," he said, gently attempting to detach the death grip on his jacket. "And far, far better than I'll be if my long-suffering valet detects any permanent damage to this coat of mine. I believe it's one of his favorites."

The woman let go of his coat with a laugh, threw her arms around his neck and gave him a quick kiss on the cheek. "Oh, Kit, my knight in shining superfine. I knew you'd come through." She stepped back and brushed vigorously at his sleeves. "There," she said with more optimism than accuracy. "Good as new."

Christopher looked down at the rumpled material. "I have very grave doubts that Jenkins will concur. However, given your anxious state of mind I will endeavor to take the blame like a man rather than casting it where it so rightly belongs. In the meantime, if you can overcome your hoydenish ways for a moment, allow me to introduce you to…" he paused for a second, aware of the amused ears of the groom who had come to take the reins and the butler standing scandalised at the top of the marble steps. He frowned suddenly at the sky. "Heavens, is it coming on to rain again? Quickly. Inside." Taking one woman's arm in his right hand and the other's in his left he dashed up the steps and through the door.

"Some refreshments in the drawing room, I think, Branston," he called over his shoulder as he marched the ladies across the entrance hall toward a panelled door on the left. "And see to the luggage, please."

Caroline, content to let Lord Saxon take the lead in his own house, remained silent at this rather high-handed treatment, but his other companion was less lenient.

"Christopher! What on earth are you doing? Let go of me at once." She attempted without success to wrench her arm away.

"In the drawing room now," Christopher said quietly between clenched teeth, dropping Caroline's arm and pulling the door open. Given little choice, but throwing a fulminating glare in his direction, she swept through the doorway and turned abruptly, crossing her arms resolutely.

What she might have been about to say was forestalled as a look of horror swept across her face. "Is Michael really all right? You weren't dragging me in here to break some awful news in private? Oh, my God! This isn't my new daughter-in-law, is it?" She seemed to really see Caroline for the first time. She looked her up and down like a sceptical buyer at a dodgy horse fair.Taking in her respectable attire and sensible bonnet she remarked, "You certainly look better than I expected. But I take leave to tell you nonetheless that I cannot approve of this marriage. Michael is only eighteen and not at all ready to settle down." Her chin came up. "And you look too old for him in any case."

"Oh, stop making a cake of yourself, Eleanor," Christopher interjected. "Of course this isn't your new daughter-in-law. I told you I'd settled everything and in any case if she was Michael's light o' love, why the devil would I bring her here?"

"Well, who is she then?" Eleanor asked with obvious bewilderment.

"I suppose you were almost correct," Christopher said with a quirk of his lips. "This is your new sister-in-law."

"What?!"

"Lord Saxon, stop it at once." Her brogue more pronounced as she spoke firmly, Caroline had quickly taken the measure of Christopher's sister and clearly decided that enough was enough. "I'm no such thing, as I'm sure your sister realizes, though how she should do so I don't know." She held out her hand and smiled reassuringly. "How do you do? My name is Caroline Saxon and I'm afraid we're in a bit of a coil. Christopher's told me all about you and I do hope you can be persuaded to help us."

For the first time the other woman seemed to stop and think before speaking, studying Caroline once again. Caroline doubted she looked her finest after an early start to her day and a long ride in an open carriage, but she hoped for the best. There was nothing she could do about it at this stage after all, so she dismissed her concerns from her mind and returned the woman's perusal with interest. For her part, Caroline saw a petite woman not in the first blush of youth who nonetheless did not appeared to have developed the sense of gravitas that middle age frequently bestowed. By the fine wrinkles that crinkled around sparkling blue eyes currently narrowed in speculation, she judged her to be a few years older than her brother. Everything about her, from the flattering cut of her fine blonde hair to the dainty slippers that peeped out below a dazzling confection of a morning dress, was clearly of the first stare. Though envy was far from her nature, Caroline, remembering Christopher's easy dismissal of her practical nature, wondered if perhaps, with a little help from her ersatz sister-in-law and the bevy of attendants she clearly commanded, she too could present a less…prudent appearance. Perhaps, she conceded for the first time, there was something of value to be gleaned from a trip to London after all.

A smile suddenly broke on the woman's face.

"Well, if you're not trying to entrap my son and you've been caught up in one of Christopher's escapades then of course you need help," she said. "I'm Eleanor Westmore and, as you seem to have gathered, I'm Christopher's sister. Do let us sit down and you can explain it all to me. I assure you, nothing you say can surprise me." She gestured welcomingly toward a gilt encrusted settee and perched on the edge of a chair in front of it while directing Christopher toward the door with a dismissive wave of her hand.

"Do see what's keeping Branston, Christopher, while Miss Saxon…how curious!…explains everything to me."

An amused look crossing his features, Christopher pulled the door open to find Branston with one hand outstretched ready to turn the knob. Behind him a young maid with an enormous silver tray waited patiently. "Ah, there you are, Branston. What took you so long? Just bring everything in and pop it on the table. We'll see to ourselves. And, ah, Branston, we're not to be disturbed."

"Very good, my lord," was the impassive reply.

When they were alone again and the tea distributed, Christopher and Caroline did their best to explain to Eleanor the events of the morning and the evening before.

Eleanor listened without interruption, contenting herself with the occasional raised eyebrow as her only commentary on the convoluted tale. When they had finished she turned to Christopher and remarked, "I must say, it seems quite foolish to have allowed Annabelle Winthrop of all people to discover you. She's a complete pea goose and she won't take kindly to Miss

Saxon's appearance on the scene. She's been setting her cap at you forever."

"I didn't exactly do it on purpose," Christopher was stung to reply.

"On purpose or not, it's got you into a great deal of difficulty which could have been avoided if you had taken more care."

Recognizing the signs of temper on Christopher's face, Caroline interjected quickly. "Indeed, Lord Saxon did everything he could. If not for his quick thinking, we would have already come to ruin. You really cannot blame him for the presence of Miss Winthrop in the same inn where we were staying."

"Nonsense, I can blame him for anything I wish. I've been doing it since he was a baby and very handy it's been as well. It's one of the only advantages of having a younger sibling."

The fond smile she bestowed on her brother precluded any sting Caroline, less used to the ways of siblings, might have imagined such a comment implied, as did Christopher's bland acceptance of her outrageous assertion. Though she had watched, and frequently envied, the comfortable, if often fractious, interaction between the brothers and sisters she'd played with as a child, she clearly had much to learn about family relationships when adulthood was achieved.

"However, I suppose there's nothing we can do about it now," Eleanor conceded, magnanimously. "But mind, Christopher, I'll expect you to take a great deal more care the next time you break into a respectable woman's bedroom."

Christopher's grave bow was belied by the twinkle in his eye. "I shall certainly endeavor to do so."

"Good. That's settled then. Now, let us decide what is to be done from here on in. I'll tell you one thing, Kit. You may be able to pull the wool over society's eyes, but you'll have to take Branston at least into your confidence. You'll never pull off such a deception within the house and success beyond these four walls would be much more likely with him on our side."

"Yes, I believe you are right," Christopher conceded. "We haven't really worked out the details yet."

"Then let us do so now," Eleanor replied.

Caroline soon had myriad reasons to be grateful for Eleanor's presence and whole-hearted commitment to the cause, not least of which was her grasp of the practical issues that would confront them. Sensible though she may be, the mechanics of organizing sleeping arrangements that would appear reasonable for a married couple but not compromise her in any way were not something Caroline would have thought to come up with. Everything from who paid for her needs, including the increased and fashionable wardrobe a newlywed would be expected to sport, to who gave the servants their orders was gone over under Eleanor's capable supervision.

"That should do for now," Eleanor finally concluded, rising with a determined air from her chair. "I'm sure we've overlooked plenty of things, but I'll have a chat with Branston, whom I assume is frantically in the midst of preparing the guest room and silently if vehemently cursing you, Kit, for not giving him any notice that it would be necessary to do so." She paused at the door for a final sally. "I can just imagine his disapproval when he realizes he'll have to prepare the mistress's room instead. If I can't turn him up sweet, you'll have to step very lightly for the next few days."

Her exit left a silence in the room. Caroline sat silently waiting, but Christopher was restless, picking up and replacing the small ornaments that graced the mantel and fiddling with the stack of invitations that lay on a tray beside the now discarded teacups.

"Is something the matter, my lord?" Caroline finally asked.

Christopher started and frowned at her as if he had momentarily forgotten her presence in the room.

"I...I'm only now realizing how dashed awkward this is for you. It seemed the only way out of our predicament when we embarked on this crazy scheme, but now I realize, stupidly, because I should have realized it from the beginning, how very much at my mercy you are. Until Eleanor started talking about the sleeping arrangements I'd given no thought to the spot I'd be putting you in by forcing you to take up a wholly untenable position in my household." He stopped for a minute, searching for words that suddenly seemed to have escaped him.

"Your room will be right next to my own and your only protection my good intentions and honor as a gentleman. Whilst I might know full well that protection is all you need, indeed you couldn't be safer if twenty duennas inhabited twenty rooms lying between our own two and all of those rooms locked with the most cunning of locks, it seems a tenuous rope to cling to for a woman who has known me for considerably less than twenty-four hours. And all because I didn't have the good sense to find my own room in a simple country inn."

Caroline thought for a minute before replying. It was obvious that Lord Saxon was feeling the weight of their position as well as a degree of guilt for the part he had played in placing them in that position. But it was a little late for qualms. They had embarked on their course and there was no turning back now. Nonetheless, she couldn't help but appreciate the fact that his real concern seemed to be for the spot it placed her in—a position of vulnerability she had fully recognized from the start.

"My lord," she finally said, her voice low and deliberately confident, almost dismissive. "You are coming to learn a fact of life that most women are made aware of at a very young age. Members of the so-called weaker sex spend their lives clinging to that tenuous rope, whether alone at a coaching inn or surrounded by family. It is only the constraints of society and the personal honor of the men around us that protects us and allows us some modicum of freedom."

"If that is indeed the case, how can you bear it?" The words burst from his lips almost before he realized he was speaking.

"How can we not bear it? It's a fact of life and we must accept it as well as we can. What alternative do we have? We are easily overcome physically, and unless we wish to spend our lives with a pistol ever primed in our reticules we must make the best of it."

It was an aspect of the relationship between men and women that Christopher had never considered before. It was so easy to talk about 'the weaker sex' without thinking about what that actually meant. To romanticize, indeed idealize, women as gentle, delicate creatures who needed to be protected from every harsh wind and the slightest physical exertion. Too many men of his class took gallantry to its extreme, regarding women as equally inferior in their minds and hearts as they were physically weaker than men, and looking upon those who weren't afraid to exhibit any kind of thoughtful, rational behavior—any evidence of thinking at all—as freaks to be either mocked or ignored.

He realized that it made no sense at all. Though they implied it was the entire sex they meant when they talked about women as delicate flowers, it was really only their own class. No one worried about the delicate sensibilities of a washerwoman or whether the scullery maid should be hauling buckets of coal at the crack of dawn. No one asked a farmer's wife if she needed help carrying the pails of milk she collected or churning the butter.

And no one asked a young chambermaid if she wanted to be kissed or not. Or worried about what became of her afterward.

Yet, weren't these women fundamentally the same as the women who inhabited the rarified atmosphere of the upper levels of society? If pricked, did they not bleed? If poisoned, did they not die? A washerwoman could become a duchess. And a duke's daughter could become a washerwoman.

And really, when he thought about it, the entire idea of men as superior beings because they possessed greater physical strength was ridiculous. He could no more stop a raging bull or outrun a herd of angry wildebeest than the redoubtable Miss Saxon. And he imagined she would be able to pull him out of the way of a runaway horse as efficiently as he could perform the same service for her. Especially if they were placed on an equal footing. But gentlewomen had been confined to foolish clothing and given few opportunities to develop their physical strength beyond gentle walks in the park or easy riding—probably making them much weaker than they needed to be, or were meant to be.

The only thing he could really protect her against was men. And, if he was completely honest with himself, not even all of them. The result was an idiotically elaborate collection of societal rules designed to keep women safe from half the members of their own species. It should fool no one. At least no one who bothered to think about them. He certainly hadn't until this minute. He imagined most men hadn't—and most women had.

It was a sobering thought.

"I assure you, Caroline, and I mean this from the bottom of my heart, in this house you are perfectly safe. Whatever guard you are used to raising, whether you realize you are doing it or not, can be safely lowered while you are under my roof. I'll never harm you, or even touch you except in the most respectful way, and I'll ensure that everyone who crosses the threshold treats you with the upmost respect. You have my solemn promise."

Before Caroline could respond Eleanor bustled back into the room.

"Well, that's settled. Goodness, I had no idea I had such a talent for persuasion, but Branston is now firmly committed to playing his part. What are you both looking so solemn for? I've managed everything beautifully."

Chapter Six

The news that Christopher Saxon, nobleman and extremely eligible bachelor, had come home from his travels abroad married to a mysterious Irishwoman of uncertain antecedents took the *ton* by storm. Newly launched young debutantes who had hoped theirs would be the charms that would finally lure him into matrimony bemoaned the luck—for surely that's all it could be—of the successful claimant to his hand. With a figurative shrug they regretfully, but optimistically— being young and sure of their own charms—turned their attention to the next candidate on the carefully ranked but never-to-be-admitted-to list of prospective husbands. Those young ladies past their first season who had been lucky enough to meet, or even share a dance and some conversation with Lord Saxon felt the news more keenly, but generally recognised that they had been accorded their tilt at the windmill and failed. So they, too, mentally moved on, although with perhaps a touch more desperation. Mothers, with few exceptions, were less sanguine, muttering darkly about tricks and contrivances and planning to watch the swell of the young viscountess's curves very carefully over the next couple of months. They'd know what to think if a 'premature' baby arrived within the first months of marriage. Their lack of knowledge about when the marriage had actually taken place did not deter them in the slightest.

In any event, those hoping to catch an early glimpse of the young lady, if lady, indeed, she turned out to be, were doomed to disappointment. Neither Lord nor Lady Saxon was home to visitors and they accepted no invitations. All agreed it was most vexing. Eleanor, who was not similarly secluded, found herself besieged on all sides. Close friends encountered at the lending library and nodding acquaintances met at musical afternoons were equally eager to gobble up any tidbit she was willing to drop into the begging bowl of their insatiable curiosity.

"I haven't enjoyed myself so much in ages," she said one evening at dinner as she regaled Christopher and Caroline with some of the more pointed enquiries she'd been subjected to that afternoon during a stroll through the park. "Lady Marsden actually drew up in her carriage to offer me a place beside her so we could have a 'little coze'. She hasn't had a kind word for me since she caught me flirting with her remarkably stupid but quite handsome oaf of a nephew over twenty years ago. I was quite floored and as a result ended up ensconced beside her before I could collect my wits about me and manage a polite denial. After a bare minimum of pleasantries, she dove right in, asking about 'dear' Lord Saxon and telling me how happy she was to hear he had wed. I assure you, I could feel her teeth grinding behind the smile."

"Why the deuce does Lady Marsden care about my marital state?" Christopher asked while helping himself to the asparagus and refusing the jellied calves' foot. "I barely know the woman and can't remember the last time I spoke to her."

"That's exactly what I was wondering, Kit! And then I remembered that she has a pretty little goddaughter she's very fond of who's enjoying a small degree of success in her first season. You wouldn't have met her since you've been away, but I guarantee Lady Marsden had her sights firmly set on reeling you in for her darling the minute you got back to town. You've put her nose out of joint with a vengeance, and I expect her only consolation is the fact that at least it wasn't some other debutante who wrested you away from her Charlotte."

Caroline laughed at the expression of distaste on Christopher's face. "It sounds like a great deal of nonsense to me. How could she possibly be disappointed when this goddaughter of hers has never even met his lordship? Is there that great a shortage of men in London?"

"Eligible men, yes," Eleanor said. "Eligible men with a title, fewer still. Eligible men with a title and enough money to afford all the elegancies of life? Now you're truly in the realm of the rarified. And eligible men who look like Kit—for even if I do say so myself he's a handsome rascal—practically impossible to find. I assure you, once this furor dies down my invitations will be cut in half as hostesses realize they can dispense with a single woman past her prime when she stops being the gateway to such an eligible *parti*."

"If you come to find your invitations are declining in number perhaps you should give some consideration to the possibility that it's your ridiculous chatter that's driving them off," Christopher interjected.

"No, but I'm sure your sister is right." The picture Eleanor had painted had struck a chord with Caroline.

She could so clearly see herself as one of those poor unfortunates had her life turned out more conventionally. "For most of these girls marriage is the only path forward. Think how bound they are. How few options they have. Even if they weren't unfit for any other occupation, societal rules preclude them from pursuing anything except what they have been taught to believe is their destiny—marriage, children and running a home. All other considerations aside, a husband with greater attributes than simply being from the right family and able to provide a minimum of financial support to a growing family must be considered a prize worth winning indeed."

"Really, Miss Saxon, I cannot argue with you when you put it so eloquently," Christopher acknowledged. "But I must say that I'm beginning to sympathize with the studs you hope to acquire for your horse breeding facility. It sounds so very cold-blooded. Do I have no other value at all?"

"I'm not saying you have no other value," she said, with the suspicion of a kind glint in her eye—or was it a sardonic one? "But as far as matchmakers are concerned it's your breeding and your ability to carry that breeding on into the next generation that principally matters.

"Thank you. If I had prided myself on retaining the slightest bit of distance between myself and your stallions my delusions have been completely dispelled by your observations."

Caroline apparently felt no sympathy. "Well, it's no different for those poor girls. How many of them are rejected because they're too short or they have a distant relative who's touched in the upper works? Those are simply traits a man looking for a wife doesn't want to see recurring in his own offspring. Yet they might be the most likeable, kindest and intelligent of women. If you are the stud, they are surely no more than brood mares when it comes right down to it. And at least gentlemen are allowed other pursuits when they discover they have absolutely nothing in common with the person they have chosen to share the remainder of their life with. Women are not so lucky."

"Goodness, I do believe this conversation is getting most improper. I'm quite sure I should put my foot down. I do stand as chaperone, however ridiculous that sounds under the circumstances," Eleanor said before Christopher could respond. She didn't sound too distressed as she gently changed the subject. "And, Christopher, please remember to call Caroline by her first name. I know we like to think the servants are just so much furniture, but really they are people and they love to gossip every bit as much as their betters. I can't imagine what kind of chatter would result if the ones that weren't in our confidence heard you calling your wife by her maiden name, not to mention what our friends would think if you're still doing it when she's ready to make her bow to society."

Christopher was clearly feeling disgruntled and being chastised by his big sister didn't help. "I still fail to see why we must hole up in the house for a week before going out into society. Surely a day or two to supposedly recuperate from our vaunted return from Europe would be sufficient."

"If Eleanor feels that we must wait a week then we must wait a week. And you are hardly restricted in your movements, my lord. You were out most of the day. It is only I who must stay indoors," Caroline pointed out.

"If I have been out it has been as much for your sake as for my own," Christopher pointed out in turn. "The terms of your aunt's will must be understood before we embark on a public display of marriage. What if there were a snag of some sort? I have simply visited my solicitor's office to ensure your compliance with her wishes will be satisfied by our somewhat unusual arrangement. I assure you," he added with a rueful smile that managed to be charming nonetheless, "an afternoon spent in the company of Mr. Fossett is no walk in the park."

"A walk in the park isn't all it's cracked up to be either when one encounters Lady Marsden," Eleanor interjected darkly.

"What did Mr. Fossett say" Caroline asked. "Are we safe?"

"He said a great deal." Christopher's lips curled down at the memory of the long afternoon spent in the dry office in the city. "And I fear he will have a great deal more to say. He bid me leave the will with him so he could go over it more closely and send his clerk out to tackle the archives for any precedents— congratulations on having the foresight to bring it with you, by the way. I'm to return the day after tomorrow to hear his final pronouncement. However, I am guardedly optimistic about the outcome. He's too fusty to commit to an opinion without a night to sleep on it and a stack of dusty old tomes to justify it, but he couldn't come up with any reason why our arrangement wouldn't fulfill the requirements of the will as it's written. He's a canny old soul and while he may find our situation morally repugnant he has nothing to say against it legally, which is all that really matters."

"Indeed, it would be a great relief to know that I won't lose by our predicament. I have no mind, after all this is over, to be forced to start from scratch without even the wherewithal to provide myself with a roof over my head." Though the words were dire, Caroline spoke them with her usual placid brogue. Histrionics and drama formed no part of her character and she had no wish to unsettle her hosts by dwelling on might-have-beens and possibilities.

Christopher looked startled by the very idea and Eleanor couldn't help but exclaim. "Caroline, you can't for a moment imagine that Christopher would allow you to suffer materially from this *contrempts*."

"Well I can hardly hang on his lordship's sleeve for the rest of my days." She paused, apparently absorbed in the study of the food set on her plate. "Although I suppose I might accept a loan to get me started. At a reasonable rate of interest, of course."

"Don't be ridiculous. As if I would do something as ungentlemanly as loan money to a woman I've to all intents and purposes ruined. What can you be thinking?"

"I'm sorry, my…Christopher." She looked at him with a dubious expression. "Would you prefer some kind of partnership? I don't think you would take much interest in the daily running of a horse breeding facility, but perhaps we can work something out if it comes to it."

"Of course you'll work something out," Eleanor exclaimed. "And the something you'll work out is a real marriage. My dear, to give you the word with no bark on it, Christopher has ruined you. If we can't pull this off the only alternative is a real wedding."

It can't be said that Caroline's jaw dropped, but a look of astonishment crossed her face. She turned to Christopher as if inviting him to refute his sister's words. She got no such satisfaction.

"You don't really believe we'd turn you out to the wolves, do you?" he asked gently. "Eleanor is absolutely correct. You are a lady and I am a gentleman. If we fail in this charade, then a real marriage is our only other option. I'm convinced you realize that I would insist upon it. My God, I assured you only the other day that no harm would befall you whilst you resided under my roof. Harm to your reputation is as great a disservice as any other and I will not under any circumstances allow that to happen."

There was no longer any doubt about the expression on Caroline's face. It was pure astonishment. "But I don't want to marry you. I have my own plans. And surely you have no desire to marry me. The idea is absurd."

If such a fervent declaration of her unwillingness to marry him hurt, Christopher gave no indication of it, except perhaps in the dryness of his tone of voice when he replied. "Indeed, there is no question of anything else. I thought you realized that from the start."

"And that's why we have to make sure we do everything absolutely right," Eleanor interjected. "You neither of you act like a newly married couple. You must learn to be comfortable in each other's company before we start parading you before all the old quizzes at Almack's and elsewhere, or they'll be sure to suspect something. That's why we've put it about that you're under the weather after your travels and can't yet receive visitors."

"But aren't people in society often married with very little acquaintanceship? They surely cannot exhibit a great degree of comfort with each other."

Eleanor pooh-poohed her objection aside. "That's completely different. The only way we can get away with this is if people think it's a love match. Why else would Christopher have married a complete unknown in such a mysterious way? No offense meant, my dear, and I hope none taken, but if the two of you don't come across smelling of April and May, they'll assume you tricked him into marriage. And that's the last thing we want if we're to be at all comfortable—or even occasionally off our guard."

"Good God, how awful that would be." The look of revulsion that crossed Caroline's face matched the one Christopher was wearing.

"Exactly," Eleanor exclaimed triumphantly. "So you must do just as I've planned. Start sitting beside each other on the sofa in the evening so you get used to being close. Christopher, you must be as attentive as possible. Take Caroline's hand in your arm and for heaven's sake, look at her occasionally! And I don't want either of you to even think about looking at the other without a smile rising to your lips. Remember, you're the sun and the moon and the stars to each other—at least for the first year."

"Eleanor," Christopher remarked, dutifully smiling across at Caroline before continuing. "I had no idea you took such a jaundiced view of matrimony."

"On the contrary, my imaginings are so romantical that it pains me to see how often couples who previously couldn't bear to be out of each other's sight can barely stand to be in the same room once the realities of wedlock have made themselves felt." She smiled brightly. "Christopher, don't linger over the port. I want you and Caroline to get in some dancing this evening so you feel comfortable in each other's arms before you attend Lady Robinson's ball on Friday night."

"So we will be allowed to go out eventually?" Christopher teased.

"Lady Robinson's ball will be your debut—if you pass scrutiny," she admonished. "In the meantime you must spend time getting comfortable with each other."

"Surely we can go for a walk in the park or something else less socially taxing?" Christopher asked.

"If you think going for a walk in the park isn't socially taxing you've been away much too long. I absolutely forbid it, if only on the grounds that Caroline doesn't have a thing to wear."

"I knew I'd have to purchase quite a few things when I arrived in town, but I've certainly brought some clothes with me," Caroline argued. "Why can't I wear them until the rest of my wardrobe is ready?"

"Because, while perfectly suitable for a young lady making her curtsy to society for the first time—and I give your maid or aunt or whoever was in charge credit for selecting a range of very appropriate items to begin with—they're no good at all for a young matron who's just returned from the continent. You're supposed to be a married woman and you'll look a good deal more dashing than you do now by the time the horde of dressmakers we've had in the house the past few days is finished with you."

She turned to her brother. "And speaking of the

ball, you'll have to go to the bank, get mother's jewels, and take them to Rundell and Bridge to see if they need cleaning or repairing before the ball. Better do it tomorrow."

"Yes, Eleanor." Though he spoke meekly enough, the gleam of amusement in his dark eyes was apparent as he turned to Caroline. "We're clearly just foot soldiers in this campaign of my sister's, so I suppose there's no use arguing."

"Excellent, you've come to your senses," Eleanor applauded as she rose from the table and signalled to Caroline to do the same. "Now don't linger over the port."

Chapter Seven

Caroline couldn't help but be thankful for Eleanor's whole-hearted support. The older woman had thrown herself into the cause not just with enthusiasm but with a practical appreciation of the pitfalls that lay in their path and a grasp of how to avoid them that Caroline completely lacked and Christopher would never have considered. As Eleanor herself admitted, she hadn't been on the town for over twenty years without gaining some understanding of what could and could not be accomplished within the limited constraints that society imposed.

"Think of it as similar to attending a masked ball," she suggested when Christopher or Caroline seemed to grow tired of her coaching. "It's all pretense until midnight when you'll be able to show your true colors again. Until then, though, you mustn't let anyone suspect what's hidden under the domino."

Caroline had never been to a masked ball, or any other kind for that matter, but she recognized the sense behind Eleanor's words. And the fact that she had never been to a ball only underscored how necessary it was to rely on her faux sister-in-law to steer her along the correct course.

Nonetheless, she couldn't help but voice a protest over the number of items of clothing Eleanor was ordering from the remarkably snobbish Frenchwoman who now seemed to be in control of her wardrobe.

"Surely I could make do with fewer dresses. Must I truly have one dress for morning and another for afternoon? One for walking in and one for riding in a carriage? It seems vaguely ridiculous," she was finally moved to protest.

"Of course it's ridiculous," was Eleanor's immediate response. "Who ever heard of having only one walking dress or one morning dress? My dear, when you're changing your dress four or five times a day it would be simple cruelty to expect your maid to maintain a single one of each style, not to mention what the other ladies on the strut would think."

Caroline wasn't impressed by this argument. "Does it truly matter so much what they think of my wardrobe?"

"Well, you don't want them to think badly of Kit, do you?" Eleanor asked as she perused the latest issue of *La Belle Assemblee* looking for tips and inspiration. "They would, you know, if they thought he was being cheeseparing with your clothing allowance. Either that or they'd wonder what you'd done with the money he'd given you to spend. In that instance, rather than thinking him a miser they'd consider him a gullible fool."

Of course that ended the argument. Caroline had to concede that spending Christopher's money with what seemed like reckless impunity was better than harming his standing in society. Although she didn't dare say such a thing to Eleanor, whose squeals of disapproval she could readily imagine, she firmly intended to repay every penny expended on her wardrobe as soon as she came into her inheritance.

And as the clothes began to appear in her bedroom she had to admit that even for someone like herself, who had never bothered much about fashion or suitable attire, there was something very pleasing about knowing one was well-dressed and attractive. Between the two of them, Eleanor and Madame Bellevue were creating a wardrobe that not only fitted her for the most fashionable of functions but suited her extremely well in the bargain. It was amazing what a flattering cut and color could do for one's confidence.

Coming out of her room one evening after changing into one of her new evening gowns, which she had learned was fancier than a carriage dress, but nothing like as elegant as a ball gown, she paused at the top of the stairs to look down on Christopher standing below her, casually leaning against the balustrade, apparently lost in thought. He, too, had changed his attire. His blue, close-fitting coat stretched elegantly across broad shoulders. From above she could see the ruff of his white shirt and gleaming cravat, as well as the faint lemon tint of his embroidered waistcoat. Even from this perspective his legs were long and lean in buff colored breeches and his hessians, since they were dining informally at home, were polished to a high enough gloss, she was sure, that one would be able to see one's image reflected in the surface.

Caroline was just giving some thought to the effect such a sight could have on an impressionable and maidenly heart, when some noise or movement must have alerted him to her presence above. He turned quickly and the expression that swept across his face caused her to momentarily forget to breathe. He clearly considered the hours she had spent over the last few days being prodded and poked by a variety of milliners, maids and hairdressers worth every excruciating second. Seeing the gleam of admiration in his eyes, she was rather inclined to agree with him.

Her hair was now cut in the latest fashion, rather than being collected neatly but unimaginatively at the nape of her neck, and the dark, shining curls framed her milk white cheeks. Her eyes glowed in the light from the chandelier above like the moon reflected on a clear ocean twilight and her slightly parted lips were dark and wet. Her gown, cut low, molded itself to her curves and though she had initially balked at the expense of new underclothes as well as new outerwear, she now realized how much they enhanced the outward appearance.

She took a deep breath and lightly started down the staircase, and Christopher slowly, as if unwittingly, started climbing toward her. They met a few steps from the bottom and he took her hand, his coal black eyes gleaming into hers as he raised her hand to his lips.

"You look lovely," he said, and there was no doubting his sincerity.

"Thank you, my lord," was all she could manage.

"Christopher," he whispered, flickering an eyelid at her in secret amusement.

"Christopher," she said obediently.

He drew her hand through the crook of his arm and continued to hold it with the other as he escorted her toward the drawing room. "Eleanor is already down and waiting for us."

"I'm sorry. I didn't mean to be late."

"When the results are this lovely, you can take all the time you like," was the immediate response.

"Eleanor be hanged."

Caroline laughed. "I don't believe you would dare say that in her hearing.'

"And you'd be absolutely right," Christopher agreed. "One of the disadvantages of having a sister some years one's senior is that one is raised, by her, if by no one else, to do exactly as one is bidden and never, ever, question her authority. I'm still terrified to death of her and always will be," he said as they went through the doorway.

"If you're talking about me, I never heard such a rasper. And I've heard quite a few from you over the years." Eleanor, seated by the fire, was every bit as elegantly turned out as Caroline, in a burgundy gown that hugged her figure and made her look not a day older than twenty-five. "You were spoiled to death as a baby and continued on the same ruinous course throughout your childhood. I assure you, Caroline, nothing is worse for a young fellow than being born years after his parents have given up any hoping of producing an heir."

"Well, you did your best to dispel any impression of privilege I might have somehow retained."

"Nonsense. Despite myself, I spoiled you as badly as anyone. I'm quite ashamed. The only reason you turned out as well as you did is because I occasionally managed to restrain myself, something mother and father never accomplished."

"Any spoiling I may have received at home, and I admit to nothing, was soon knocked out of me at school."

"And a very good thing as well," Eleanor responded promptly. "You would have been completely insufferable otherwise. Now I believe dinner is ready. Shall we retire into the dining room?"

It was some time before Caroline was able to fall asleep that night. She could not deny she found Christopher a very attractive man. She had done so the first time she saw him in the filtered firelight of her bed chamber and the harsh light of day had done nothing to dispel her feelings. But, here under his roof, seeing him every day, her attraction to him was growing. And she now had reason to suspect that he might not be completely indifferent to her either.

She did not delude herself into believing Christopher's feelings ran deep. Fine feathers and a fashionable look could do wonders to attract a man's attention. At least that had always been her aunt's contention and she now saw that this was indeed the case. With the exception of one rather tepid compliment on the road to London, Lord Saxon had behaved with complete propriety—almost indifference, although she admitted he was a perfect gentleman at all times, and never let her see how little interest he had in her as a woman. She had told herself that was fine. She had told herself repeatedly, she admitted to herself. The last thing she or her plans for the future needed was the complication a relationship developing with a man like Christopher would bring.

But tonight there had been something in his expression that had more than once made the heat rise to her cheeks. During dinner, she had felt his eyes on her as she looked down in silence at her own plate. And afterwards as they practised dancing together under Eleanor's watchful eye, the feel of his hand on her waist was hot with a warmth that had nothing to do with the temperature of the room. While his attraction might be a momentary response to her fine new appearance, it was dangerous.

With a restless sigh she rolled onto her side and told herself once again that Christopher Hawkins's likes or dislikes were no bread and butter of hers, and the sooner she stopped thinking about him the better. It didn't help. She finally fell asleep remembering the glint in his eye and imagining them twirling together in an impossibly large ballroom surrounded by stars.

It was most unusual.

Chapter Eight

Christopher gave the reflection in the mirror barely a glance as his valet fussed around, making the final adjustments to his appearance before allowing him to emerge from his dressing room into the public eye.

"My lord, please be still," Jenkins tutted as he swept away an invisible crease and frowned at the perfectly cut cloth of the black jacket that hugged Christopher's body like a lover. "Even if you don't have your pride, I do. It's known I have the dressing of you and no one's going to see you turned out in anything but perfection on a night like tonight, if I have to tie you to the chair to do it."

"Using my own cravat to do so, I imagine. Such a course of action is unlikely to produce the effect you're after, I would have thought," Christopher replied, momentarily diverted from his own impatient thoughts by his valet's pleas.

"Just so, my lord." It was clear Jenkins was not amused. "So perhaps you would be good enough to stand still for one minute more and spare us both the ordeal."

Christopher stopped fidgeting obediently, well aware that he was still in his valet's black books for haring off after his nephew without him, not to mention coming back in as great a pickle as Jenkins, who had been with him since he came down from university, had ever seen him in. But his thoughts were far from the cut of his coat or the sweep of his hair, however artfully they had been arranged. Tonight was the ball to which he would escort his sister and Caroline.

Over the past few days, he had come to know Caroline in a way that would have been impossible under other circumstances. The constraints of social interaction were such that men and women spent very little meaningful time together. Chatting whilst performing the two dances allowed per ball or meeting for a few heavily chaperoned minutes in the park were often the best that could be managed under ordinary circumstances. Even members of a house party specifically designed to alleviate the boredom that some found stifling out of the season were not constantly together the way he and his ersatz wife had been.

Eleanor was absolutely correct in her assertion that the two had to become completely comfortable with each other. Any shyness on Caroline's part or standoffishness on his would be remarked upon with gleeful speculation by the members of the *ton*, who generally speaking, had very little else to do but comment on the doings of everyone else. Though they would deny it to their dying breath and appear shocked at the very suggestion, a titillating *soupçon* of scandal was exactly what they hoped for. But, failing that, they would get what mileage they could out of dissecting his and Caroline's every move. He would be fooling himself if he tried to believe that everything about them wouldn't be under scrutiny, from the clothes Caroline wore to the way she tipped her head when listening to someone speak. They would decide on a whim whether her face was beautiful, whether her carriage was graceful, whether that whiskey-smoked voice was pleasing to the ear. And, once pronounced upon, they would stick to that decision come what may. If the collective decision was in her favour, her path would be a relatively smooth one. If it was not, it would take a duke's approbation to bring her into favour.

He would be subject to a different but equally penetrating examination as the quizzes and beaus tried to ascertain how he had been changed by his sudden marriage—and whether it was for better or worse. Was he still the same Lord Saxon they had come to, if not love, at least regard as a familiar and welcome member of their exclusive ranks? Would he still participate in their doings, or was he, they would shudder to think, ready to retire in domestic bliss? Living under the cat's paw would make him much less amusing and that, to a bored and limited society, would be the worst crime of all.

The result had been several days of almost complete isolation as the two got to know each other's likes and dislikes, habits and eccentricities—not that either admitted to having any such things. It represented a strange stillness before the storm and Christopher, to his complete surprise, found he resented its conclusion. He had enjoyed getting to know Caroline, learning, just as he was meant to, what it signified when her chin came up or her brogue became more pronounced.

Getting physically comfortable was something different entirely. As she became more natural at sitting close to his side or casually putting her hand on his arm as they conversed, he felt himself becoming more stilted, more unnatural. Her closeness overpowered his senses. The fact was, he had never been more attracted to a woman. There was something about her that drew him. He might have been tempted to blame the unusual closeness into which they had been thrust, except that he suspected she would have commanded his attention across a crowded ballroom or from the other side of Hyde Park.

Eligible man. Eligible woman. The prescribed path forward seemed, to all intents and purposes, clear.

Be damned if it was.

It had been a shocking revelation to Christopher to discover that in this day and age women considered themselves so vulnerable. His conversation with Caroline on the first day of their arrangement had troubled him deeply. The last thing he wanted was for her to feel threatened or constrained in any way. Yet his position as the rich nobleman in whose house she was sheltering lent him a degree of power that could not be ignored. They could not meet under his roof as equals, much as he might wish to assure her that he had no intention of taking advantage of her. Much as he might never, in word or deed, actually take advantage of his position.

To declare any kind of romantic interest in her under these circumstances would unequivocally be the act of a rogue, regardless of how honourable his intentions were. Even if she had the spirit to refuse him, and he firmly believed that if anyone in such circumstances did it would be Caroline, he would make her dashedly uncomfortable. If that weren't bad enough, he doubted very much whether they would be able to continue on with their charade after such a confrontation. So after all their preparation and efforts she would be ruined anyway, forced to leave London under a cloud and without the inheritance she so desperately needed. And he would be painted as a villain of the first order, from whom all eligible girls would be justifiably sheltered by vigilant mothers terrified their own darlings would be similarly compromised.

And if she accepted his advances, he doubted that the situation would be much better. A part of him would always feel he had used her unfairly, taken advantage of her vulnerable position and coerced her, even if he did it with charm rather than pressure, with finesse rather than intimidation. He would wonder if she really loved him, if she would have accepted him in other circumstances, if she would have shared his feeling had they met on a ballroom floor, in the park, over dinner.

On top of everything else, no matter how happy their future path might turn out to be, no matter how blessed their marriage, he knew he would always feel that he'd let the side down. Proven to Caroline that, indeed, even with the best of intentions, men were incapable of mastering their more brutish natures. Unable to allow an attractive woman to reside under their protection without claiming her as their own.

He just couldn't do it.

Which left him with no possible path but to keep his feelings—and his hands—to himself. To ensure she did not suspect for a moment that his feelings for her were more than those of an acquaintance, more than those even of a close friend. He would treat her with courtesy and respect. He would allow her hand to rest on his arm as they spoke and never let her guess how he longed to draw it into his grasp, dance her around the

Barbara Burke

ballroom with the requisite distance between their waltzing bodies, his hand gently touching her waist in guidance only, without letting her discover how much he longed to close the distance and pull her near, their bodies touching.

Christopher had always been grateful to have been born into the modern world rather than the brutal times his ancestors roared around in. But being a sophisticated and civilized gentleman of the early nineteenth century had suddenly become a burden. Not that he wanted to thunder down on horseback, throw Caroline over his saddlebow and ride away with her to a no doubt extremely uncomfortable stronghold of solitude like some medieval marauder.

Not exactly.

And certainly not if she wasn't participating in the fanciful abduction with an enthusiasm to match his own.

But if she was…

He sighed regretfully. He was a sophisticated and civilized gentleman of the nineteenth century, there was no getting away from it, and he would never behave in such a deucedly ill-bred fashion.

Besides, he didn't have a stronghold of solitude.

His reveries were abruptly interrupted by the sound of raised voices coming from outside his room. Raising an eyebrow at his startled valet he strode toward the door and pulled it open. Though the voices hadn't sounded angry, they were unusual in his generally placidly run household. Except, of course…

He leaned over the railing at the top of the hallway and took in the scene below him with more resignation than surprise. From his vantage point he could see his long suffering butler slowly disappearing underneath a pile that consisted of, as far as Christopher could gather, Venetian tanned gloves, a ridiculously high brimmed beaver hat and a coat with more capes than even the most *tonnish* Corinthian was like to sport, all the while being subjected to a nonstop list of instructions from the person doing the piling up.

"Michael! What the devil are you doing here?" he called down.

The commotion and chatter came to an abrupt halt as the slightly built young man, who seemed to be somehow taking up most of the space in the foyer, glanced up sharply.

Forgetting all about his admonitions to Branston on the proper care of his greatcoat he bounded up the stairs, taking them two at a time in his eagerness.

When he reached the top and stood facing Christopher, it would have been apparent to even the most casual observer that the two were related. Though he still sported the slenderness that indicated he hadn't yet reached full manhood, he shared Christopher's height and dark intensity, as well as his easy air of authority.

But the indignant expression on his face was all his own.

"What the devil do you think I'm doing here?" he demanded.

"If I knew that I wouldn't be asking. Less than ten days ago I pulled you out of a scrape fit to ruin you. Was it my imagination that you promised to behave until the end of term? Because, now I consider it, it does seem unlikely I could ring such a concession out of you. Have you been sent down?" He carefully left the "again" off the end of the sentence, but it hung between them, nonetheless.

"Well, if that don't beat the Dutch!" Michael frowned in indignation, his voice rising. "I come racing down at a most inconvenient time, I don't mind telling you, to see if I can help you out of some sort of scrape and all I get is abuse, and…and…dashed aspersions cast against my character. A fellow may as well let his uncle go to the devil in his own time and spare himself the trouble if this is the kind of reception he gets."

Seeing that his nephew was truly upset, Christopher spoke mildly. "Well, I don't know what this is all about, but I can see you have only my best interests at heart. I was just getting dressed. Come into my chambers and tell me what you think the problem is before your mother gets hold of you." He ushered the young man along as he spoke and gently closed the door to his room behind them.

A decanter of brandy sat on a small gated table and, after gesturing his nephew toward a chair by the fire, he went over to pour two glasses of the rich, dark liquid, handing one over before settling himself in the other chair and dismissing his valet.

"Now what's this all about? What sort of scrape do you imagine I'm in?" he asked carefully.

"That's what I'm trying to find out," Michael responded. The indignation in his voice hadn't abated and it was clear he was not going to be fobbed off with brandy and a warm fire. "Not a fortnight ago you're lecturing me on the folly of getting caught in the parson's mousetrap, and practically before my ears have stopped ringing, I'm learning from some fellow at school, who shouldn't be the one to have to inform me, and dashed embarrassing it was, I'll tell you, to be standing there like a complete cawker while everyone seems to know everything about my family's business except me, that you've been leg-shackled in what I can only conceive of as a very havey-cavey manner. All this without a word to me, who, you might think, would like to know when he's suddenly been thrown out of the succession and, probably, the only home he's had practically forever." He paused for effect before delivering the final volley. "Not to mention what's going to happen to his poor widowed mother."

At that Christopher couldn't restrain a crack of laughter. "Since your father left her as well off as any woman has any right to be, I imagine that if she were indeed thrown out on to the street, which I believe is what you're implying I'm about to do, she'd set herself up in one of the more fashionable areas of town and decorate it to the nines, the way she's been trying to do with this place for years."

"You know what I mean."

"Yes, indeed." There was a twinkle in Christopher's eye. "But don't worry, I'm sure she'll find it in her heart to allocate a corner of the garret to you for dining on your bit of crust, and storing the few rags you're allowed to clothe yourself in."

"Dash it, Uncle Kit, stop trying to bamboozle me." Michael's youth was suddenly and painfully clear as he attempted to keep his voice level, but Christopher could see the hurt he was trying hard not to let shine in his eyes. "I'm not a child."

Christopher studied his nephew carefully. He sometimes underestimated the degree to which Michael had grown up in the last couple of years, and the fact that he continued to get into scrapes he needed rescuing from didn't help. But it had to be admitted he was getting older and the sort of scrapes he was now getting into reflected that. Running off to get married was a considerably different kettle of fish to playing schoolboy tricks on the headmaster. And even were that not the case, Christopher was forced to admit, the fat was in the fire now. He really had no choice but to take his young relative into his and Caroline's confidence.

"No," he said. "My apologies. The fact of the matter is, Michael, we're in a bit of a coil. I thought we could leave you out of it, but I was clearly mistaken. I'll have to tell you the whole and rely on your discretion and your desire to help. But, before I go on, I need your word that what I'm about to tell you will go no farther."

"Well, I like that!" Michael, while willing to be talked round, was clearly not completely mollified. "What kind of loose-jawed cake do you take me for? Of course I won't say anything."

"Thank you," Christopher answered meekly. "Naturally I know you're completely trustworthy, but there's a lady's reputation at stake and I cannot be too careful."

Michael's eyes gleamed.

"Don't tell me you really have been trapped into marriage by some fair plotter."

"On the contrary, the trapping was all mine," Christopher replied, and began to tell Michael the story.

Chapter Nine

Christopher was, perforce, brief in his explanation. Not only were the details none of his nephew's business, but Caroline and Eleanor would be waiting to attend the ball. Given the mysterious way news seemed to move through his household he was surprised his sister had not already banged on his door, demanding immediate access to her one and only child.

He had barely recited the details, and endured a great deal of whooping at his expense, when the knocking he had expected threatened to tear the mahogany door off its not inconsiderable hinges.

"Christopher, open this door immediately!" came ringing from the hallway. "Townsend tells me that Michael is come home. Oh, do let me in. Whatever can be the matter now?"

Christopher looked across at his nephew and nodded his head. "You'd better let her in. She's not going away."

Michael got up from the chair he'd been half lounging in and half sitting on the edge of as he listened to his uncle's tale and opened the door that his mother continued to pound on.

"Hello, m'dear," he exclaimed in a casual tone, drawing her into a quick hug. "I'm just here to find out what the deuce Uncle Christopher's been up to. Can't be too careful, you know, and clearly you've got no control over him."

"Oh, Michael." Vexed as she tried to sound, the brightness of her eyes and the firm clasp she took of his hand told a different story. "Are you truly not in any trouble at all?"

"No, dash it!"

It was clear he was about to set off into a litany of his grievances again if Christopher did not forestall him.

"Michael has simply been concerned about some rumors he heard in college about his suddenly disreputable uncle. I've been filling him in on what's been going on."

"Oh, Christopher, we should have thought of that." Eleanor exclaimed. "We were so busy ensuring things would go smoothly here that we completely neglected to consider that naturally word would get around elsewhere. Oh, dear. I wonder who else is about to descend on us demanding answers."

"Let's hope that, unlike this bright sprig here who apparently has nothing better to do with his time, the majority of them confine themselves to writing testy letters."

"They probably will," Eleanor said with some relief before suddenly pausing. "Except perhaps Aunt Hilda. We must write to her immediately for she'll descend on us in the blink of an eye if she thinks we've done anything behind her back and I really don't think I could cope with her right now, not to mention her smelly dog who is constantly in need of being taken for a walk around the square, and her dusty old lady's maid who always treats Townsend as if she were a lightskirt who thinks she's better than she should be."

"Yes, but never mind all that." Michael was clearly impatient with hypothetical arrangements for antiquated relatives, no matter how much the thought of them might terrify his mother. "When do I get to meet my artificial aunt?"

"Right now, I should imagine. Caroline is amazingly prompt and we were to assemble in the withdrawing room at 9:30, which has just struck. Come downstairs and be introduced. Unless you want to freshen up first." Christopher looked his nephew over carefully, pointedly taking in his disheveled hair and muddy boots.

"Not a bit of it! I can't wait to meet her. She sounds like a sensible girl and won't mind me in my dirt, I'm sure."

"Let us descend, then."

****

Caroline felt as though she were a mannequin under the capable but forceful hands of Townsend, lent to her for the evening by Eleanor, who wished to ensure that not a single flaw could be found with her appearance. Primped and prodded like a piece of wicker work, her only role seemed to be to stand still and allow herself to be dressed. However, when she was finally permitted to look in the mirror she could find no fault with the machinations of the formidable dresser.

The deep red of the dress should have washed out her fair coloring. Instead it darkened her hair even further and make her skin glow like cream in a sunlit jug of the thinnest porcelain. It was not a color she would have been allowed to wear as an unmarried debutante and she couldn't help a *soupçon* of gratitude to steal over her that here at least was one advantage to her debut in deception. The cut of the dress was of a kind similarly restricted to married women, clinging to her form and forcing her breasts to appear ready to pop out of their precarious restraint. She had never dreamed she could look so...dashing, so...dangerous.

"His lordship sent these up, madam," Townsend said, pulling out a strand of gossamer gold interspersed with rubies and pearls, apparently indifferent to the revelations Caroline was experiencing. "I told him what colors you would be wearing and he chose from the family collection accordingly." Whilst there wasn't any suggestion of approbation in the maid's voice, Caroline knew quite well that the necklace would not have been presented if it had been deemed lacking by this arbiter of all things appropriate.

"It's lovely," she exclaimed, holding the string up to the light.

"It'll do," Townsend admitted grudgingly. "And there's earrings and a bracelet to match."

The jewels added the finishing touches to what was already the most beautiful outfit Caroline had ever worn. She wondered if they were recognizably part of the Saxon family collection, in which case Christopher might well be making a Machiavellian gesture to trumpet her legitimacy as a new member of that family. Cunning though it might be, it somehow made her feel even more of a fraud. However, she also had to recognize that wasn't going to stop her from wearing the jewels. It was simply a practical demonstration of her position, she told herself firmly, and she'd raise suspicions and eyebrows if she balked at wearing the family jewellery. The fact that the rubies and pearls lay against her skin like a lover's caress was immaterial. As was the realization that she wanted desperately to see if she could once again spark that look of admiration in Christopher's eyes.

Completely immaterial. Her life was definitely complicated enough. Definitely.

"Thank you, Townsend," she said in her usual calm tones. "You've done a perfectly wonderful job of turning a sow's ear into a silk purse. You should be proud of yourself."

Townsend stood a little straighter and her pursed lips almost smiled. "Not quite a sow's ear, my lady," she said. "Just a woman of small experience who might need a little help showing herself off to her best advantage."

"You've worked miracles nonetheless," Caroline insisted.

Townsend's lips regained their usual thin line. "Not me, ma'am, that's the job of the lord." And with those words their brief moment of rapport was at an end.

Caroline was surprised to hear voices coming from the withdrawing room as she descended the stairs. There sounded to be a lively discussion taking place, and one of the voices was unfamiliar to her. She paused when she reached the main floor, wondering who might have appeared who would be so clearly welcome even if unexpected.

"Don't be ridiculous, darling." Eleanor laughed affectionately, and the identity of the mysterious newcomer was instantly made plain. It must be her son, of course. Bracing herself for introductions, Caroline carefully gathered her demi-train and entered the room. She moved quietly and the attention of the three occupants of the room was centered elsewhere. Nonetheless, Christopher's head immediately turned toward her as she stepped through the doorway.

He smiled warmly and came toward her, holding out his hand to take hers and lead her forward. "Caroline," he said. "Let me introduce my reprobate of a nephew to you."

She saw before her a handsome young man who had not yet achieved the full height and breadth he one day would, but who was still well on his way to manhood. His resemblance to his uncle seemed at first slight, but when he smiled and came forward, a welcoming smile on his face, she immediately recognised the relationship.

"My dear Aunt Caroline," he exclaimed, grinning as he bent over her hand. "How very pleased I am to meet you at last. I've heard so much about you from my reprobate of an uncle."

"All right, consider me duly chastened," Christopher said before retrieving Caroline's hand and leading her to the settee. "Michael has been berating me for not telling him of our marriage earlier. He knows the whole story now."

"The whole story?" Caroline asked.

"Yes indeed." Michael quickly took a seat next to her. "You can be assured I will do everything I can to further the cause and ensure everyone comes out unscathed."

"By which he means he's short of funds and consequently loathe to get on my bad side. Any *further* on my bad side," Christopher concluded meaningfully.

Michael made a face in his direction before turning back to Caroline. "You have my deepest sympathy," he said, matching his uncle's tone.

"Thank you," she replied, the twinkle in her eye belying the gravity of her voice. "But I'm sure your deepest sympathy won't be necessary."

"Yes, do stop talking nonsense, darling. Caroline will think we're a very odd family indeed."

"More so by the minute."

"And that's enough out of you as well, Christopher," Eleanor continued, unfazed. "Good heavens, sometimes it's difficult to tell which of you is the elder."

"I'm simply responding to provocation," he interjected.

"But I do know which one of you should be more ashamed of such childishness," she carried on as if he hadn't spoken. "Now someone pour Caroline a glass of sherry immediately or we'll be late for dinner and cook will start throwing pots again, which is extremely disconcerting for everyone else in the kitchen no matter how justified his behavior may be."

Caroline was amused. "I hardly think throwing pots can be considered justified behavior except perhaps in the most extreme circumstances."

"Yes, my dear, of course you don't, but you're not a man, are you? Their behavior is quite often completely unaccountable, I assure you."

Thoroughly chastened both Christopher and Michael leapt to do her bidding, and the ten minutes before they were called in to dinner passed without further incident.

Unless spoken to directly, Caroline remained silent through the meal. They had done everything possible to ensure that her rather unexpected entry into society would go off smoothly, but she still felt a degree of trepidation. It wasn't just her own reputation that would be sunk without trace were things to go ill. These three people she shared the table with, who were chatting away to each other with clear affection and who had welcomed her into their fold without hesitation, would also face ruin. They wouldn't just be humiliated; they would be unforgiven. Society might accept the most *outré* behavior, but there were limits, and the masquerade they were embarking on was firmly outside that limit.

She watched Christopher as he spoke to his nephew, laughing over some shared memory to the evident disapproval of his sister. His face was open, his eyes alight with amusement and his mouth curled upwards as if he hadn't a care in the world. Yet he was seated at the table with a woman who could ruin him with a few brief, but oh so damaging words. Of course she would find herself equally ruined. But the stakes were definitely lower for her, with no expectations of ever taking her place in society, and a home to return to where the members of her restricted little community were as oblivious to the goings on and opinions of the *ton* as any inhabitant of the outermost reaches of the British Empire.

On the other hand, any misbehavior Christopher was discovered in would eventually be forgiven, no matter how scandalous. As Eleanor had pointed out, he was young, single, titled and rich, all characteristics guaranteed to redeem him eventually, no matter what the circumstances.

And he was awfully good-looking.

Of course, a harelip and the temper of a hastily

roused badger wouldn't stop some desperate mothers from considering him a prize catch. It was the way of the world when marriage was the only chance most girls had of escaping a life of poverty and a sense of failure, dependent either on a resentful male relative for the very bread in her mouth, or her own exertions in one of the woefully few occupations open to females.

Really, she thought, in some exasperation, Christopher Hawkins should be a little more careful of who he invited into his house to pose as his wife. It was a situation ripe for exploitation. If she didn't have a perfectly good future mapped out for herself that didn't involve a handsome nobleman who had once looked at her as though she were the most desirable creature on the planet, she would pose a real danger to his continued bachelorhood.

Sometimes being a sensible woman who played fair was the very devil.

"Caroline, have you finished?" Eleanor's voice brought her back to her surroundings. "The carriage has been ordered for half past ten and it's just that now. We really should be going."

"Of course," Caroline replied, rising to her feet before either Christopher or the footman had the opportunity to pull out her chair. "I'm quite ready to go if you are."

"Let's get our wraps then," Eleanor said and led the way out of the dining room.

The carriage ride was a brief one, mostly taken up with Michael's repeated assurances that everything would go splendidly and his vows to throw himself into the breach if they didn't, while his uncle wondered aloud why he had so little faith in Michael's ability to improve a difficult situation.

As Christopher handed her down from the carriage, he took the opportunity to ask her quietly if she was feeling nervous.

"Not at all," she replied calmly, although she could feel the butterflies in her stomach and was having difficulty unclenching her hands. "We have done everything we can to ensure things go smoothly and now it is time to put our preparation to the test. The battle is about to commence and having an attack of nerves now will only lessen our chances of victory." She lifted her chin defiantly, her eyes sparkling in the cold light of the moon.

"My sensible Miss Saxon, as always," Christopher replied and briefly raised her hand, touching the back of it with his lips in a gentle salute.

"Lady Saxon," she replied coolly, trying not to let the thrill his touch had sent scampering down her spine affect her voice, attempting to concentrate instead on the increasingly unwelcome designation sensible. Even though if there were one time to keep her head on her shoulders, this was it. "Please don't lose us the war before the first skirmish."

It was still early enough in the evening that the crush of guests lining up at the door to the ballroom remained unabated. As the four of them took their place at the end of the slowly moving queue, Caroline felt as though she could feel eyes boring into her from every direction.

"Don't worry," Michael said, cheerfully, correctly interpreting the expression on her face. "It'll get a lot worse once we're actually inside. The best we can hope for is that there'll be so many people about that very few will actually be able to see you past the crowds."

"Are you somehow under the misapprehension that you're being helpful?" Christopher growled.

"Boys!" Eleanor warned. "You may smile. You may cultivate a look of ennui. You, Christopher, may even try for a degree of doting affection socially acceptable only on the face of a newlywed as you gaze at Caroline. But no one will look worried or apprehensive. Is that perfectly understood?"

It was.

Michael's ennui, Caroline's small shy smile and Christopher's doting expression were all duly on display as Eleanor swept them into the ballroom and the welcoming arms of their hostess.

"Dear Eleanor," Lady Robinson, a statuesque woman in a complex, scarlet turban exclaimed as she carefully embraced the younger woman. "You've filled my ballroom as no one else could with your promise to bring your new sister-in-law tonight for her debut in society. We are all, naturally, agog." She looked expectantly toward Caroline. "Don't just stand there like a mangel-wurzel, Saxon. Introduce me to your bride."

"Mangel-wurzel? Your language seems to have taken a turn for the agrarian since we last met."

"It could have been worse," Caroline said without thinking. "She could have compared you to a turnip."

"How could that be worse?" Christopher couldn't stop himself from asking.

"Because at least a mangel-wurzel has a bit of blood in it, my dear boy." She beamed at Caroline and held out her hand. "It's clear I'll have to make the introductions myself, since no one else seems capable of concentrating on anything but the most trivial details."

"Allow me to present my new wife, Lady Saxon," Christopher interjected before she could continue. "Caroline, this is our rather formidable hostess, Lady Robinson." He cocked an eyebrow. "Who, it seems, is playing a solitary hand tonight."

"Oh, Robinson's already wandered off into the card room. We won't see him again until supper is served, and not even then if he unaccountably takes it into his head to start winning a hand or two for the first time in his life." She laughed without malice, a big hearty sound. "It's nice to meet you, my dear. And Christopher, it's good to have you back in town, no matter how many managing mamas' noses you've put out of joint." She turned her attention on Michael. "And you, young scamp, I suppose you've been sent down."

"Not at all!" Indignation sent his voice soaring into the upper reaches and his face reddened slightly. "I'm just here to lend my uncle and new aunt a bit of support."

"Very good of you," Lady Robinson's look belied her words. "I assume your pockets are to let. A lack of funds is the only reason I've ever known a lad of your age take any notice of family responsibilities."

"Don't rise to her bait," Christopher warned before Michael could speak. "She'll have you on the ropes before you know what hit you."

Lady Robinson laughed again. "Very good advice. At least you've learned something while you've been away. Now go and enjoy yourselves, if that's at all possible with people ogling you from every direction. Perhaps we'll get an opportunity to chat later." With these words and a gentle flick of a hand, she turned to her next guests, who had been patiently waiting their turn.

Caroline had never seen so many people in one room before. There must have been six hundred people lining the walls several deep and twirling on the dance floor, the reds, greens and blues of the gowns making a kaleidoscope of color as they moved around the room.

"How does one even breathe in such surroundings?" Caroline asked. "No wonder they call it a crush."

"I believe breathing is optional," Christopher replied. "Do you wish to make your way through the throng or take a turn on the dance floor?"

It suddenly occurred to Caroline that for the first time in her life, she was on the arm of a very handsome man who, for tonight at least, would be paying her the closest of attention. She was dressed more beautifully than she could ever have imagined and looked better than she had ever done in the past. She felt a swell of...could it be recklessness?...take hold. The night held magic in its cupped hand like a gemstone.

"I want to dance and dance," she exclaimed.

Christopher grinned, as though equally infected. "Then let us do so," he said, holding out his hand.

Christopher was a wonderful dancer. Caroline should have expected it. After all, he seemed to do everything he undertook with grace and ability. A waltz was playing, and as Christopher informed her as he drew her toward him, since she was a married woman, even though only now making her entrance into society, she needed to ask no one for permission to dance it in the arms of her husband.

And Christopher was doing a very good job conveying the appearance of a doting bridegroom. In fact, if Caroline didn't know better, she would swear his expression was genuine. His eyes held a gleam that seemed to be only for her and his lips softened when she spoke. Their surroundings, the heated crowd and fevered chatter, seemed to recede as they danced until Caroline was aware of nothing but Christopher, the feel of his hand holding hers, the warmth of his broad shoulder under her gloved hand, and the touch of his palm against her back as he guided her through the swirling throng. She was grateful to be a woman, grateful that it was his task to lead. Had it been left to her, no one else on the floor would have been safe. She would have danced right into them, oblivious to their very existence.

She was jarred back to reality when the music stopped and Christopher stilled their twirling steps.

"You dance beautifully," he said, a touch of wonder in his voice.

"Thank you. You sound surprised."

He led her through the crowd, his hand gentle against the back of her waist. "Let's get something to drink," he said before continuing, "Actually I suppose I am. I didn't really think about it when Eleanor made us practice in the parlour. There was hardly room for more than a few steps. From what you've said about your upbringing, I would have thought lessons with the local dancing master would have been very low on your aunt and uncle's list of priorities."

"You'd be quite right to so presume," she agreed. "However, Eleanor made sure to get someone to give me a few lessons so I wouldn't look completely out of my element. I'm glad I didn't make a total fool of myself."

"You give yourself to the music in a way that is as delightful as it is unexpected. It's a pleasure to dance with you."

Caroline could feel a blush creeping across her skin, a curse someone of her complexion learned to live with from an early age. It wasn't the music she was giving herself to. It was the feeling of being enfolded in Christopher's arms. She took refuge in a prosaic response.

"Thank you, but you are complimenting me under false pretences. I had nothing to do but follow in your steps."

"Well, follow me over to where Eleanor is, and I'll procure you a glass of punch."

Before they could reach their destination, however, they were interrupted by a handsome man in the uniform of a Coldstream Guard. "Saxon!" he exclaimed in ringing tones. "When did you get back? Some dashed idiot told me you'd been leg shackled. Say it ain't so."

"Waverly." Christopher grinned, clearly comfortable with this rather unorthodox interruption. "I'm delighted to say that rumor doesn't lie. Allow me to introduce you to my wife. Caroline, I'm ashamed to admit that this great oaf is a friend of mine."

Captain Waverly grinned unrepentantly. "Put my foot in it as usual, didn't I?" he said, as he made his bow. "Won't be the last time, I expect. Very pleased to meet you, Lady Saxon. Not at all surprised Saxon's become a tenant for life with such an inducement, dashed if I am."

"How do you do, Captain. It's lovely to meet one

of Christopher's friends." Caroline smiled up at the handsome soldier.

"Kept you close guarded, has he?" Waverly grinned. "Not a bit surprised. I've known him forever and he's always been bad at sharing."

"We met overseas, you clod, and have only just returned. Is there some reason you're impeding the flow of traffic through the room besides that of making a deuced nuisance of yourself?" Christopher enquired with a raised eyebrow. "Because I wouldn't want to keep you from it."

Waverly turned to Christopher with a ready smile. "Can't remember, but I might have been looking for you. Anyway, it doesn't matter. I'd much rather dance with your lovely wife." He held his arm out to Caroline. "May I?"

"Of course. You can tell me all about Christopher's childhood."

"Christopher never had a childhood. He was too busy being Lord Saxon's heir. It was a deuced serious business from all accounts," Waverly said as he led Caroline to the end of the room where a set was just forming for the next dance.

Christopher watched them walk away, Caroline's head tilted toward Waverly as he regaled her with what was no doubt some completely inappropriate and probably slanderous story. It was good to see his old friend again, even under circumstances in which he had to be less than aboveboard. He didn't like having to deceive him. There were more complications to this venture they had embarked upon than he had first envisioned and they were piling up. It was difficult in ways that were unexpected. Caroline smiled suddenly at something Waverly said, and it was as if her face was lit from within. Christopher watched her laugh as his best friend took her in his arms for the dance, regaling her the entire time with some foolishness. Some foolishness she was clearly enchanted by. Damnably difficult, he realized ruefully.

Chapter Ten

"Did you have a good time last night, my dear?"

Eleanor and Caroline were sitting at the breakfast table enjoying the quiet and sipping tea while perusing the mail and the morning papers. Both Michael and Christopher had business elsewhere, Christopher with his tailor, and Michael with showing how responsible he could be by riding in the park at the most fashionable morning hour and talking to all and sundry about his wonderful new aunt.

A smile spread across Caroline's face and a faint hint of roses crossed her ivory cheeks.

"I always used to think that so-called society was just for flibbertigibbets and people without worthier occupations to fill their time," she admitted. "But there's something about whirling around a dance floor that is quite lovely. Just as virtue is its own reward, perhaps pleasure can be enjoyed simply for the sake of pleasure."

"Well if it can't there's not much point in it, is there? Why pursue something that has no value except in what it conveys in so fleeting a manner? And yet most people do."

"Quite right." Caroline took a thoughtful bite of the piece of toast she had been carefully spreading marmalade upon. "Even if we don't enjoy our food, we must continue to eat in order to live. We merely make it taste as good as possible to make the task of eating a less onerous one. In the same way we must have shelter so we enhance our surroundings as much as possible. By making them as pleasurable as possible, we actively pursue food and shelter and thereby increase our well-being. So that might be why things we must do are things that can be made enjoyable. Following that line of reasoning, do you suppose it's possible there's a hidden but essentially practical reason why we enjoy dancing?"

"I've no idea," Eleanor admitted. "Perhaps it's a mating ritual. All cultures seem to enjoy some form of dancing, just as they all cultivate food and build shelters. And certainly mankind wouldn't last very long without some form of encouragement for the opposite sexes to mingle."

"And music, therefore, is no more than a sophisticated form of a mating call. I believe we have cracked it, Eleanor."

"Who would have expected breakfast philosophy to lead to such deep conclusions?" Eleanor placed her cup firmly back in its saucer and laid aside the letters she had been half-heartedly perusing as they chatted. It was clear the time had come for serious conversation. "Now that you've make your bow to society, things are about to get a lot busier, and with the best will in the world, Townsend can't serve as lady's maid to both of us indefinitely." She made a face that caused Caroline to grin. "And though she does wonders with hair cutting and coordinating different articles of clothing, no one could ever accuse Townsend of even a modicum of good will, never mind the best will. I've been thinking about how we're going to keep you up to snuff, as

Michael would say, and still maintain our privacy."

"I've been worried about that, too," Caroline admitted. "I had to leave my maid with my chaperone. She wouldn't have betrayed me for the world, but now I'm rather glad she's not here, even though I feel guilty for feeling so. Poor Annie doesn't have the experience or sophistication to dress someone to the standard deemed necessary for a London season in the highest circles. Her abilities were fine when I was simply here to essentially pay lip service to the terms of my aunt's will. I didn't care what I looked like under those circumstances as long as I was able to put in a respectable appearance. But the situation has changed and I cannot bring disrepute to Christopher, and indeed, to you by appearing shabby in any way, as I now realize I would do if I were to dress in the way to which I am accustomed." She laid her toast carefully aside and allowed the concern she felt to appear in her eyes. "But what is to be done? As you say, we must be circumspect. How can we hide the fact that Lord Saxon and I are not sharing a bed?"

"Well, my dear, believe it or not, Townsend has come up with the solution. One of the maids here has ambitions to become a lady's maid herself and Townsend has taken her under her wing to a certain extent. She suggests that this girl—Jane Andrews is her name—might be brought into our confidence, as if it weren't perfectly likely that the entire staff doesn't know everything about our situation, because they always do, and under Townsend's guidance and tutelage, have the dressing of you. What do you think?"

"I think it's a splendid idea."

"Excellent. Let's have her in and you can see what

you think."

Jane, or Andrews as her position as lady's maid now demanded she be addressed, was soon accepted and happily tripped off to take command of Caroline's new wardrobe.

"Don't worry, miss. I'll see she does as she should," Townsend, who had been present during the interview, assured her before marching out of the room.

Thus it was that an hour later, Caroline was dressed impeccably for a drive in the park, which Christopher had promised her when his business was concluded. There were quite a few people in the park and Caroline and Christopher's appearance there clearly caused a great many heads to come together in whispered commentary. Caroline, in a sprigged muslin gown with a matching bonnet and muff, was pleased with her appearance, glad she had a maid of her own who was able to dress her in a style befitting her false position. It was a side of herself she hadn't realized existed and, as was becoming more and more natural, she turned to Christopher to share her insight.

"You know, my lord…"

"Christopher," he admonished.

"Christopher," she corrected herself with a slight tilt of her chip straw bonnet. "I cannot make up my mind whether I am more amused or bemused by my enjoyment in bedecking myself in the latest fripperies of fashion. It's not something I ever would have considered myself to have a weakness for."

"Why should you be either?" he asked. "Simply enjoy it. You look very fine."

Caroline didn't allow herself to become dejected over the rather insipid phrase. She had no expectations of Christopher waxing eloquent over her appearance.

Really.

But 'fine'? That was a word you used to describe a horse's gait.

She carried on. "But it is not something I was ever raised to consider worthwhile. This morning Eleanor and I were discussing the pleasures of dancing, and now I'm discovering the pleasure of dressing well. I fear I'm turning into a foolish creature who will soon abandon herself to gaiety and dissipation."

Christopher laughed before raising her kid-gloved hand to his lips with one hand while commanding the reins in the other. "My sensible Miss Saxon turn into a foolish creature? I wish I might see it! I think you need have no fear on that score, despite your new wardrobe and penchant for dancing."

"Am I so irreversibly dull, my lord?" Caroline hoped she didn't sound as sulky to his ears as she did to her own.

"Ah, I'm in your bad books again, am I?" He gave her hand a squeeze before returning it to her lap. "On the contrary, Caroline, I think you would make an admirable society lady, if that's what you're worried about. However, I cannot see you give yourself over to such a life completely. Your mind is too active and your habits of industry too ingrained to allow you to be content for long with what is essentially a very superficial existence."

"I'm sure I don't know whether you are complimenting me or not. You make me sound a very dull creature." Caroline was unmollified.

Christopher was taken by surprise. Caroline—his sensible Miss Saxon—had never indicated before that she considered herself to be anything other than a practical woman with little time for trivialities. Why should she suddenly take offense when he agreed with her? Did she believe there was some virtue in frivolity? That was absurd, but he could think of no other reason for her apparent pique.

"Surely you cannot imagine yourself spending your days doing nothing more worthwhile than sipping chocolate in bed and reading your correspondence before getting up and heading to the milliner's for an earnest discussion of the advantages and disadvantages of dyed chicken feathers over genuine peacock's plumes, followed by a round of drawing room visits with people you've already learned everything of interest about long since, and culminating in another crush in another ballroom indistinguishable from last night's setting, before finally heading to bed in the wee hours to do it all over again the next day? I cannot believe it of you."

Beside him, without moving a muscle, Caroline seemed to somehow swell with indignation.

"Thank you very much indeed, my lord, for pointing out how entirely unsuitable I am for the role of viscountess," she said through gritted teeth. "That is what you were saying, was it not? Or, wait, was it something else altogether? Was my behavior becoming too convincing? Was I starting to look and sound like a woman who might possibly *belong* in the upper levels of society? A woman who might possibly recognize there could be some pleasure and enjoyment in spending her life not working and scheming and planning to keep body and soul together? We mustn't have that, must we?"

Christopher's head swivelled toward her in surprise, his attention wholly taken from the carriage path in front of him. "What on earth do you mean? Your plan was, I supposed, thought out and your course laid out. Had you wished a more permanent London connection we never could have embarked on this scheme. And besides all that, you really are not the kind of woman I can see being contented for long with such a life. Indeed, I did mean it as a compliment."

Caroline didn't know why she was so angry. Everything Christopher said was true. She did have concrete plans, plans she'd worked hard to develop and which she had no intention of abandoning. And even if she did enjoy some aspects of life in London's upper milieu, it was also true that a life devoted entirely to its tenets, a life such as Eleanor seemed to enjoy unreservedly, would drive her to distraction in no time. The fact that what he said was true didn't matter. On the contrary, in ways she would have difficulty explaining, even to herself, it made his remarks that much more annoying.

"Clearly you do not understand, my lord."

It became immediately apparent that Caroline was not the only one attempting to speak through gritted teeth. "Clearly," was the somewhat strangled response. His grip on the reins tightened.

How long the icy silence would have lasted if left to their own devices was never discovered. Driving in the park at the fashionable hour was mainly done to see and be seen. The result was a good deal of stopping and starting as carriages, riders and walkers held up the traffic to ensure they saw and were seen by the right people. After the ball where Caroline had finally been introduced to society, half the *ton*, or so it seemed on a sunny morning in the park, wanted to be seen to be on the closest terms with the new viscountess.

Then there was the other half.

"Saxon," an imperious voice commanded from an imposing barouche lumbering to a stop besides their more dashing equipage. "Introduce me to this mysterious wife of yours."

"There's nothing mysterious about her, Mrs. Winthrop," Christopher replied mildly. "Unless you are trying to solve the conundrum of why she would consent to lower herself to marry someone as unworthy as myself."

"Humbug," the matron barked, the feathers in her tall, black bonnet quivering. "You well know your own worth, I've no doubt." She turned her attention to Caroline. "So this is she, is it?"

Caroline wasn't sure if she was meant to answer or not. She sat quietly and returned the elderly woman's appraising look calmly, making no attempt to speak. She saw before her a rather raddled countenance under the imposing headdress with small, dark eyes squinting suspiciously in her direction. She looked as if she smelled something foul coming out of the drains. Caroline wondered if she was naturally bad-tempered or merely shortsighted. Sitting beside her was a mousy woman unfashionably dressed, who may well have been much younger than her clothes and pinched look of anxiety suggested

"Yes," Christopher continued unperturbed. "Allow me to introduce you to Mrs. Winthrop, Caroline. You may recall meeting her granddaughter, Annabelle, when she barg...er, dropped by our sitting room at that delightful inn we stayed at on our way to town. And this is Miss Winthrop, who accompanies her mother on all her expeditions about town."

"How do you do," Caroline said, nodding to each in turn. "It's a pleasure to meet you."

Miss Winthrop's hesitant response was overborne by her mother's louder harrumph. "Annabelle said you had no countenance to speak of and even less sense of style. I don't know how I managed to engender such a pack of fools. It must have been a weakness in Mr. Winthrop's line. Well, I must congratulate you, Saxon. You could have done worse." She rapped forcefully on the side of her carriage and the large conveyance rumbled forward. As they passed from sight Caroline heard Miss Winthrop plaintively begging her mother to confine her complaints about the family *to* the family.

"What is it about members of the upper class!" Caroline exclaimed when she was sure they were out of earshot, her earlier pique forgotten. "I never know whether I'm being complimented or torn to shreds. What an extraordinary old woman. Am I without countenance and dress sense, or the complete opposite?"

"You may not understand how the game is played, but you're an excellent participant. Mrs. Winthrop would be equally befuddled by your description of her. As for her comments, clearly Annabelle was being less than complimentary and her grandmother has formed a decidedly better opinion of you. You can take that as an accolade or not as you choose. Personally, I would discount both opinions, although Mrs. Winthrop's, being positive, and therefore, all the rarer, might have greater value."

The rest of the promenade passed without incident. Caroline did feel rather like a prize cow at a county fair, but she was well aware of her status as a nine-day wonder and knew the sideways looks from under straw bonnets and whispered comments behind carefully concealing gloved hands were only a temporary phase—a stretch of the hunting ground that had to be ridden over as lightly as possible and then forgotten about. In the grand scheme of things it meant less than nothing.

Except, it was rather gratifying to learn someone in this difficult society truly thought she was up to snuff, even if it was a mean-tempered old lady who was clearly the scourge of her entire family. And when they returned to the house it was to discover a pile of cards and invitations that had been left for them, both together and separately, spilling across the mantel in the drawing room. It was abundantly clear that for the next several weeks, if they so wished it, they would not be forced to spend a morning, afternoon, dinner, or evening alone together. Caroline was a success.

Chapter Eleven

Two weeks later, Caroline wondered how most members of society managed to maintain their sanity. She and Christopher were like carriage horses, sharing a stable with the best of everything and prancing side by side day after day, but always in tandem and facing forward, barely able to make eye contact, ruthlessly bridled and never allowed to rest except late at night in their own separate stalls, equipped with everything they could wish for except companionship.

Caroline had never before realized how lonely a horse's life must be.

"How on earth do you manage it year after year?" she asked Eleanor in frustration one morning in a rare moment of quiet as they walked to the lending library to choose books they wouldn't have time to read. "I feel like I haven't had a rational conversation in ages. I've practically forgotten what a sensible remark sounds like, never mind the sheer bliss of actual silence."

"Oh, my dear, I knew I shouldn't have allowed Bucky Buckingham to snabble the dinner dance with you last night. He never had two thoughts to rub together even as a child, according to Christopher, who went to Eton with him, of course, and he seems to be getting worse every season. Everyone says his mother was a complete pea goose, so he probably wasn't given many brains to start with."

"It's not just Bucky. I'm quite used to him," Caroline assured her. "And I've learned how to brush him off if I need to. You no longer have to be quite the nursemaid I needed when we started this venture."

"No, my dear. You're doing beautifully. Just the other day Lady Robinson told me that marrying you was the most intelligent thing Christopher had done since he came down from Oxford, and I couldn't help but agree with her."

"Except he didn't, did he?" Caroline said gently.

"Didn't what?"

"Marry me."

"Well, there is that," Eleanor admitted. "But Lady Robinson doesn't know that and I try my best to forget it, too, so I don't slip up."

"But the point is, how do you manage? I feel like if I hear one more whispered confidence about the probable parentage of Lucy Langford's coming *petite package* I'll start howling like one of the monkeys at the Tower zoo."

"It is the height of the season. It's not like this all year round. Well, there's also the little season, to be completely fair. But people do retire to their estates quite regularly and London can be extremely thin of company during the summer and over the hunting season. In October I can go weeks without attending a really good party unless I'm staying with friends in the country."

"It sounds like heaven!" Caroline exclaimed as they reached their destination and ascended the steps to the front door.

Eleanor laughed as she opened the heavy wooden door. "You say so now, but just wait until you're reduced to inquiring after the well-being of the housekeeper's great nephew just to keep her tarrying in the drawing room a little longer."

"You forget," Caroline replied as she loosened the buttons on her burgundy pelisse and stripped off her kid gloves. "I was practically raised by our housekeeper and played with all the village children. I probably knew better than she did how her great nephew was doing."

"I don't believe you. If your housekeeper is anything like ours, she's much too grand to admit to being related to any of the village children." She laid the books she had been carrying in her muff on the counter. "Do you have anything in particular you'd like to look for or shall we just browse?"

"Can we see if Walter Scott's latest novel is available? It's called *The Black Dwarf*. I know his novels are not as elevating as his poetry, but how can I resist such a title?" Caroline asked.

"Of course," Eleanor said. "I hope you have more luck than me. I'm quite convinced I'm going to be forced to actually purchase Caro Lamb's *roman à clef* if I don't want to end up being the last person in London to read it. They say the things she writes about Glenarvon, who's really Byron, of course, are absolutely libelous. Well, they would be, and really, how can one besmirch Byron's good name or reputation? He'd be absolutely crushed at the suggestion that he still had either one. It's the things she writes about everyone else I'm dying to see. Lady Jersey is so incensed she's considering banning poor Caro from Almack's."

"Goodness." Caroline had been in London long

enough to know what a pariah that would make the attention-seeking authoress. "I feel rather sorry for her. Imagine having to work that hard to get people's attention. In fact, imagine needing people's attention so desperately you'd be willing to expose your private affairs to such a degree."

"Affairs being the operative word," Eleanor agreed with unaccustomed drollery.

"Oh!" A voice piped up from behind one of the bookshelves. "Are you talking scandal? Please let me join in."

Both women turned to see a pretty, young face with a disingenuous expression peering at them. It was Caroline's acquaintance from the inn who had started all the trouble in the first place. They nodded politely.

"Hello, Annabelle," Eleanor said. "I'm not sure we were talking scandal. We were really discussing books, believe it or not."

"Oh, books." Annabelle fluttered a dismissive hand across the space between them and rolled her pretty blue eyes, clearly expressing her opinion of people who would entertain such an unworthy topic of conversation, and in a library of all places. Then she brightened. "Did you hear Lady Jersey has rescinded Caroline Lamb's entry to Almack's? Can you imagine?"

"Yes, we'd heard a rumour to that effect," Eleanor admitted. "I don't know if it's actually…"

"Oh, I'm sure it's true," Annabelle interrupted. "My sister had it on the best authority and she's seldom wrong about these things." The girl looked around before leaning forward and lowering her voice to a suitably conspiratorial timber. "She also told me she

Barbara Burke

knows for an absolute fact that the father of Lucy Langford's coming baby is…"

Hearing a snort from the general direction of her ersatz sister-in-law, Eleanor interrupted. "Really, Annabelle, I'm surprised at your sister discussing such things with you. She might be a married lady now, but that's no excuse for confiding such matters to a girl barely out of the schoolroom. I consider it most unsuitable."

Caroline took the opportunity to drift away while Eleanor was talking. She was well aware that Eleanor didn't give two pence whether or not the young girl's indiscreet sister shared the latest *on dits* with her. She was simply giving Caroline the chance to escape both a discussion of the poor child's probable parentage and the carefully orchestrated change in conversation to Caroline's own marital status that would inevitably follow. Hearing the girl chatter on so unrestrainedly, she sent up a prayer of thanks that Christopher at least had been wise enough to realize that if they had been foolish enough to confide in her during their unfortunate meeting at the inn, they would already have been embroiled in a scandal to make the question of Baby Langford's possible parentage pale to insignificance in comparison. Caroline rather doubted whether even Mr. Scott's imagination was up to the task. She very much doubted that the trials and tribulations she naturally assumed would inevitably beleaguer the hero in *The Black Dwarf* would bear comparison to the perils and pitfalls of successfully functioning in the upper echelon of London society.

Having discovered the whereabouts of Mr. Scott's latest adventure, she settled herself at one of the small tables provided to leaf through its pages. She was well into the second chapter before Eleanor finally managed to make her escape and join her.

"That girl could talk the hind leg off a donkey," she exclaimed with more truth than tact. "In another thirty years she'll be studiously avoided by all her quaking relatives and so-called friends, and never understand why they consider her such a dragon."

Caroline tried to be fair. "She certainly seems to enjoy talking about other people's business, but don't we all?"

"Not to the exclusion of everything else, no matter how it may seem when you're listening to the same story for the fourth time in as many minutes. And certainly not with such bloodthirsty enthusiasm. Her sister's just the same and don't get me started on her mother!" Eleanor visibly shook herself. "I see you found what you were looking for. I'm afraid all the copies of Caro's book are still out on loan. Honestly, it makes me wonder why I waste my pin money on a first-class subscription when they don't have the only book I really want to read available. Do you mind stopping in Hatchards? I can't bear to wait another day to find out what all the fuss is about, so I'm going to have to purchase it."

Caroline was quite agreeable to this change in plan. She had early discovered that one of the real advantages to life in London was the proliferation of bookshops and subscription libraries, and never refused an opportunity to explore their fascinating collections. By the time the ladies had made their way back to the house they were not only in possession of Lady Caroline Lamb's scandalous book, and of course, *The*

Black Dwarf, but Caroline clutched the latest edition of Weatherby's *General Stud Book* as well as *Kubla Khan,* which she purchased over Eleanor's objections.

"My dear, what a poser Coleridge is. Just trying to make himself interesting with his dreary visions and complaints about interruptions," was her contemptuous dismissal of the work when Caroline's interest lighted upon it.

Caroline suspected she might be right, but Eleanor wasn't the only one willing to pay to read a book just because she wanted to know what everyone was talking about. And the purchase of Weatherby's book helped to assuage any guilt she might have felt about such a frivolous acquisition.

She was deeply engaged in following the lineages of the recent thoroughbred champion racehorses as delineated in Weatherby's the next morning—fascinated by the information given and not at all pining for the rather lurid novel that had kept her awake far later than it should have the night before—when she was interrupted by the arrival of Mrs. Winthrop and her granddaughter, trailed by a somewhat scandalized but resigned Branston.

"Don't get up, gel," the imperious old lady instructed as she entered the room, clearly expecting Caroline to do just that. "I'm not here to take tea or sit around wasting half the morning gossiping about people who are no bread and butter of mine."

Caroline wisely ignored the command, and moving away from the table by the window where she had been seated, gave Branston the signal to bring refreshments and invited Mrs. Winthrop and Annabelle to sit down. Perching on the edge of the rose patterned settee

Annabelle looked about her with interest, her eyes lighting on everything from the ormolu clock on the mantel to the medallions on the ceiling. Remembering their first meeting and the way she had run up to clasp Christopher's hands, Caroline wondered if she was picturing what might have been, imagining herself as the viscountess entertaining guests in this, her own, no doubt completely redecorated, home.

Mrs.Winthrop, perched regally in the chair by the fire, her hands folded firmly on the silver handle of her ebony cane, seemed more intent on studying Caroline than her environs. "Still have your figure, I see," she commented.

It took a moment, and a scandalized inhalation from Annabelle, for Caroline to understand what she meant. When she did, her face turned scarlet. "Yes," she stammered. "That is…"

"Well, these things can take time. I was four years before this one's father was born. We began to despair, but all was right in the end, as my mother assured me it would be." Her gaze sharpened. "How long have you and that scamp been married?"

It was a question they had assumed would be posed by someone and they had prepared an answer, but for the life of her Caroline couldn't remember what the answer was. "Five months," she finally said. "We were married on the continent."

"Probably just as well not to be increasing so quickly, then. There's plenty of people with nothing better to do with their hands than count on them, and if they don't add things up properly that doesn't stop them from spreading any tale that will gain them the most attention. In a year or two when the dust has settled, there can be no question as to why Saxon married you." She changed the subject abruptly as the butler entered with the tea tray. "Irish, aren't you? Where are your parents?"

"Yes, I'm Irish. My parents are both deceased." Caroline poured carefully and passed a cup to Mrs. Winthrop, pleased to notice that her hand didn't shake. Clearly her visitor had no compunction about digging out as much information as she could. Caroline wasn't sure why. Passing a cup to Annabelle before settling back with her own she smiled at the older lady, resolutely determined not to be put out of countenance for a second time. "Lord Saxon and I met in Lisbon where I was travelling with my aunt. I wouldn't call it love at first sight, but others might interpret our meeting differently and our courtship was quite short. Is there anything else you would like to know?"

"I never asked anything about how or where you met Christopher. Do you think this is some kind of inquisition?" Mrs. Winthrop didn't betray her breeding enough to slam her cup down on the table, but she placed it there very firmly before sitting up even taller. Her hands returned to her cane and clutched it like claws.

"Isn't it? I must apologize. Was there another reason for your visit?" Caroline asked, a hint of amusement in her smoky voice and one eyebrow ever so slightly cocked. "Oh, of course, you wanted to see for yourself whether or not I was with child. Apparently people who cannot count aren't the only ones who are curious about my condition. I suppose you will all just have to wait and see." She directed a sideways glance at Annabelle who was sitting as if turned to stone, her mouth shaped like an "o", and her eyes wide.

For a moment it looked as though the old lady would rise up in high dudgeon and leave the house never to darken its doors again. Caroline wasn't sure whether to feel relief or dread at the prospect. But after swelling up like a pouter pigeon, Mrs. Winthrop relaxed and a small smile almost touched her bloodless pursed lips.

"You've got a tongue on you, no mistake about that," she said. "That's not necessarily a bad thing. However, be warned. There are other sharks swimming in these waters who may not be quite so ready to put up with your impertinence." She reached down for her cup and held it out with an imperious motion. "I'll take another cup of this bohea if it hasn't gone bitter while we chatted."

The door opened as she spoke and Christopher came into the room, dressed in riding clothes. He had clearly heard the last remark and breezily said: "No bitterness here, Mrs. Winthrop. Caroline wouldn't put up with it." He winked at Caroline before bending over the old lady's outstretched hand and greeting Annabelle with a smile.

"Would you like a cup of tea?" Caroline asked him as she poured. "There isn't much here, but I can send for more hot water."

"Not for me, thank you. I was just going out for a ride and wondered if you'd like to join me, but I see you are happily occupied elsewhere."

"Yes," Caroline said. "I was just telling Mrs. Winthrop and Miss Winthrop about how we met in Lisbon."

"Ah, yes." The amusement in Christopher's eyes

was only visible to Caroline. "I remember it well. You were wearing a peach-colored dress of some sort, I believe, and carrying a parasol."

"Nonsense," Mrs. Winthrop interjected in a decided manner. "I never heard such a rasper. There isn't a man alive who would remember such a detail as what a woman was wearing when he met her."

"But I remember it just as well as I remember all the details about our courtship. Caroline will bear me out!" Christopher protested, the twinkle in his eyes becoming more pronounced.

Caroline shot him a look. "Indeed," she said, turning to Mrs. Winthrop. "My husband is quite correct. I remember I was wearing a peach dress and the sun beat down dreadfully. All the ladies carried parasols, though, so he gets no points for remembering that."

"I'm sure it was love at first sight," Christopher continued, elaborating on the theme. "These have been the best three months of my life."

His words fell like stones into the suddenly quiet room.

"Five months, my lord," Caroline said. "We've been married five months."

"Have we?" He looked startled, but recovered quickly. "The time seems to fly past when I'm with you, my dear. It's amazing to think we've already been together so long."

With a sound that may have been amusement, disdain or simple arthritis, Mrs. Winthrop rose from her seat and gestured to Annabelle. "Come, girl. I've seen what I wanted to see." She turned to Caroline, who was frowning at Christopher in a way that did not bode well for his immediate future. "You may call on me. I'm generally at home on Tuesdays and Thursdays. As for you…" She turned to Christopher. "Doing it too brown, Saxon! I know when I'm being mocked."

"Not at all," he protested, as he extended a fashionably clad arm for her to take and led her to the doorway. "I wouldn't dream of such a thing."

Annabelle, who had remained silent through most of the visit turned to Caroline before following her grandmother out the door, her eyes determinedly disingenuous. "How very odd that Chri…Lord Saxon doesn't even know when you were married. One would think it would be a memorable occasion—and such a recent one as well."

"Not as recent as he seems to think." Caroline could almost hear the wheels turning in the young girl's head and laughed in as carefree manner as she could manage as she and Annabelle followed Mrs. Winthrop and Christopher out into the hallway. "But he remembers the important things."

"Well," Christopher said after their guests had been safely seen off the premises. "I'm afraid I muffed that one."

"She's a prying old harpy to be sure," Caroline agreed. "But I rather like her. I don't think any harm was done."

"Well, you're a better person than I am, there's no denying. Women like that put the fear of God into me."

"I have to admit she did get my dander up a bit, but we seem to have managed." Caroline dismissed the old woman from her thoughts. "Now what brings you home at this time of the day? I thought you were away about your business until this evening."

"Actually, I did come back to see if you'd like to

go for a ride in the park. It's a beautiful day; the sun is shining and there's no wind for a change."

Caroline's face fell. Her disappointment was palpable under the bright light that streamed through the windows above the door. In candlelight her skin had a creamy glow. In sunlight it was pure alabaster. "I'd love to, but I promised Lady Robinson I'd look over patterns with her. She wants to redecorate one of the bedrooms for when her granddaughter comes to visit next year. It's her coming out and Lady Robinson wants to show her she's being treated like an adult, not a schoolroom miss."

Christopher startled her as much as himself by moving closer, and taking her left hand in his right one. His dark eyes blazed and his face wore an expression Caroline was afraid to interpret, a look she had thought she had seen on his face once before when she was dressed for dancing and he had stood watching her slowly descend the stairs. A look that told her he was seeing her in a way that made her skin tighten and brought a delicate flush to her cheeks. But today there was no candlelight, no change in her appearance to catch his attention, no expectations. Just the two of them mercifully alone.

"I don't suppose there's any possibility of your telling Lady Robinson to go hang, is there?"

His clasp on her hand tightened and the sapphires in Caroline's eyes gleamed with regret. "I'm afraid not. I made a promise. I can't back out for something so frivolous as a canter in the park, however brightly the sun might shine."

"No, I suppose not." Christopher said, slowly lifting the hand he was still holding. The touch of his lips on her palm was feather soft, but Caroline felt its reverberations to the tips of her toes. "It wouldn't be sensible."

"No, it wouldn't," she managed to say.

He released her hand gently. "What about tomorrow? Bright and early before the responsibilities of the day have an opportunity to come between us and any plans we might make to spend some time together."

"I'd like that," Caroline said in her soft, smoky voice. Their eyes locked and it seemed as if a silence, a certain stillness, hung upon the air. Caroline found herself catching her lower lip with her teeth, expectant but unsure. She watched Christopher intently, saw his breath catch. Without volition she raised her head slightly, bringing her face closer to his and made a small, tentative, and wholly involuntary movement toward him.

And then she watched him withdraw from her, creating distance between them without moving a step.

"I'll have the horses brought round in the morning, then," he said tightly, and left without a word or look back.

Christopher spent the rest of the day, and all of that evening, at his club, trying not to get too drunk and not succeeding particularly well. It didn't go unremarked that for the first time since the onset of his sham marriage he was somewhere other than at Caroline's side. But he endured the rather heavy-handed teasing with a grim smile and silence. Naturally, this led nine out of ten of the men in the room to assume Lord Saxon and his wife had just had a dustup of biblical proportions. They were newlyweds. It wasn't unexpected. Chuckles all round.

Captain Waverly, who had come upon Christopher enduring a sincere talking-to by one of the more senior and stentorian members of White's about the folly of giving fillies their head this early in the game, had whisked him into one of the quieter lounges and rung for a bottle. The two sat silently for a while, swirling the claret in their glasses and contemplating their own booted feet stretched out before them toward a welcoming fire.

"Nice woman, Lady Saxon," Waverly said at last.

Christopher grunted in reply.

"Attractive, too," his friend added helpfully.

Christopher repeated his last response.

"And reasonable. Doesn't seem like the type to start flinging crockery at one's head or anything."

Christopher shot him a long look under lowered brows. "Are you going anywhere with this, or are you just compiling a list of attributes for your own amusement?"

"Don't know," Waverly answered, unperturbed by Christopher's unwelcoming tone.

"Then perhaps you'd best keep your own council until you figure it out."

It was Waverly's turn to grunt, albeit in a more agreeable manner.

Christopher poured himself another glass of wine and with an air of resignation signaled to the attendant to bring another bottle.

"Caroline is wonderful," he finally said. "That's the problem."

Chapter Twelve

The sun had consented to reappear in its full glory early the next morning and the few clouds that hung puffily and decoratively in the sky remained firmly fixed, unruffled by the frequent cold winds that too often ruined a winter's day. The air was brisk and the ground was soft without being muddy. It was a perfect day for a ride in the park.

Caroline and Christopher were not the only ones to take advantage of the fine weather. Despite the early hour, the bridle path in Hyde Park was packed. Groups, men alone and women, either with escorts or grooms trailing discreetly behind them, walked, trotted and cantered up and down Rotten Row, paying small heed to the grooms out exercising the horses of those members of the ton too slugabed to ride their own horses, but paying very careful attention to each other.

What they made of Lord and Lady Saxon was anyone's guess. The pair rode side by side, Caroline on a silver-maned gray mare that was rather larger than usual for a lady's mount and Christopher on a long-legged roan with a tendency to forget he was no longer a stallion and behave accordingly. Christopher was attentive in every way possible, helping Caroline into the saddle with quiet dexterity and keeping between her and any rider who looked even remotely less than capable of controlling his or her mount—certainly nothing he needed to worry about with Caroline, who had an excellent seat and the firm, gentle hands of a first-rate rider. But there was a formality to his actions that contrasted sharply with the warmth he had exhibited the previous afternoon.

Caroline still could not understand the change that had come over him as they stood together at the bottom of the stairs in the Mayfair house. One minute he was treating her in the way she was increasingly coming to realize she wanted him to treat her. As someone special, someone important. Someone desirable. The next he was a polite stranger, his manners impeccable and his touch without emotion. He had greeted her that morning with a stiff smile that conveyed no warmth and didn't quite reach his eyes. His hands as he'd guided her into the saddle might as well have been assisting— she tried to imagine with whom he would exhibit such cold courtesy—Mrs. Winthrop!—into a chair. His shoulder, when she lay her hand on it to steady herself as he boosted her up, was unyielding as granite.

When they reached the end of the bridle path they stopped a moment to look out over the park before them. Winter wasn't the most flattering season for an area dedicated to long swaths of mown grass and towering deciduous trees. A few hard frosts had lent a gray cast to most of the vegetation. But there was a stark beauty in the sinuous branches and limbs of the great trees, twisting up to the sky, naked and exposed to the elements.

Caroline turned to Christopher on impulse, an eager expression lighting her eyes to an almost azure shade as she patted her horse's neck. "May we ride out under the trees?" she asked. "The ground looks firm enough, no one's strolling on the grass and my poor Princess is pining for a gallop."

Christopher's expression warmed slightly. "Yes, if it would please you. I feel much the same way as poor Princess and I'm sure this old fellow could do with the exercise."

Caroline almost grinned. "I'll race you to the third elm," she cried over her shoulder as she picked up the reins in both hands, crouched lower in her seat and urged her mare forward.

Christopher wasted no time giving his own horse his head and the happy gelding jumped ahead as eagerly as his more ladylike stable mate.

They reached the stand of trees much too quickly for Caroline's liking. It felt like she had only just begun to experience that sense of flying that was the best part of racing on horseback, riding *ventre-a-terre* as her great-aunt used to scornfully describe it. But her great-aunt, for all that Caroline had truly loved her, had been the kind of woman who would always prefer more cerebral activities. For all of Caroline's practical nature, she also embraced the sheer physical pleasure of movement for movement's sake. Riding was like waltzing, as she had discovered in the ballrooms of London. You moved in tandem with a partner and there were certain prescribed and hard-learned patterns that needed to be followed. After that, though, you gave yourself over wholly to the movement of two bodies in sync, and the result could verge on the subliminal.

"I win," she cried as they drew to a halt at the base of the designated tree, their horses' feet stamping on the ground as they reluctantly halted.

"I fail to see how you can make such a claim when

I'm right here beside you," Christopher protested, his expression lighter than it had been all morning. "At best you managed to keep up with me."

"My lord…!" Caroline exclaimed as Christopher muttered, *sotto voce*, "I knew that was coming."

"My lord," she repeated with a quelling look. "Clearly, since I watched you ride up, I must have gotten here first."

"You watched me ride up, but your vantage point was not, as you claim, here, but considerably farther back. Admit it, you watched me from behind," he teased.

Caroline swelled with indignation. "You, my lord,"—"Here we go again."—"are no gentleman!"

Christopher's chuckle was deep and genuine. "And you are definitely a lady, so I suppose I'll have to admit defeat even if all the evidence suggests otherwise. You are a capital horsewoman so it's quite possible that you could have beaten me."

"*Could* have beaten you? My lord, I don't know how you can say such a thing with a straight face!"

"No, I assure you, you ride magnificently." Christopher's face rearranged itself into the picture of innocence.

The look Caroline gave him would have been recognized by any of the village children she had quelled into submission as a young hooligan. The corner of Christopher's mouth twitched and Caroline had difficulty maintaining her stern expression.

"Well, perhaps it was a tie," she conceded.

"Indeed," said Christopher. "Even Solomon would have no difficulty accepting such a judgement. Let us call it a tie."

It was too cold to stand idly for long. The steam rising off the horses was indication enough that they needed to keep walking or risk giving their mounts a chill by allowing them to cool down too quickly. By mutual consent they walked their horses along the line of grass that ran beside the trees, keeping to the firm footing the lawn provided.

Away from the bustle of the official path and the scrutiny of the other riders, the world was a quieter, more bucolic place, even in the heart of London.

"Oh, this is grand." Caroline took a deep breath and held her face up toward the weak winter sun, her eyes closing and the shadow of her lashes darkening the alabaster of her cheeks. "I hadn't realized how much the relentless bustle of constant social engagements was getting me down. I feel as if it's been weeks since I've taken a breath of air that hasn't already been shared by a dozen other people."

"Yes, it can certainly take its toll, especially if you're not used to it. And even though I was raised to spend half the year in London, I always breathe a sigh of relief when I get back to Hawkings and wonder why I ever leave it."

Caroline turned to him curiously. "Then why do you leave it?"

"Believe it or not, I do feel a certain responsibility to my position. I took my seat in the House as soon as I was old enough and I attend the sessions regularly."

"Am I in the presence of a future minister of state?" Caroline asked.

"Absolutely not. That would entail too much time spent in town. I need to feel my own soil under my feet at regular intervals."

"Ah, now you're sounding like an Irishman," Caroline exclaimed, purposely broadening the brogue that was never very far beneath the cultured tones in which she generally spoke. "You'll be after pining for a tot of good whiskey next."

Christopher laughed. "Well, to be fair, it's not just duty that brings me back. Man is a social animal, and I enjoy visiting my club and even doing the pretty in society to a certain degree. More to the point, my tailor has never expressed the slightest desire to wait upon me anywhere else but in the confines of his own shop on Bond St."

"Ah, that is a compelling reason!"

"I think so."

Their meandering had taken them to the edge of the tree belt and they stopped for a moment to gaze down on the ice forming on the Serpentine.

"Shall we go round to the deer pound?" Christopher asked. "Perhaps the sight of some forest animals will cure our homesickness, or at least our *ennui* with London."

Caroline was glad to see that he seemed to have overcome whatever had been bothering him earlier, and willingly agreed. They rode slowly, guiding their horses gently in the right general direction, but allowing them to keep their heads low and relaxed. Princess whickered softly at something only she noticed and Christopher's roan answered her agreeably.

"How big is Hawkings?" Caroline asked. "Am I about to learn that I've not been treating you with the deference your position in the country deserves?"

"What? When you drop 'my lord' into the conversation as often as others say 'Your Majesty' when speaking to the king? Pray spare me your deference if you think you haven't been paying me enough. Hawkings is large enough to suit me very well, but by no means what you might term a pile. It started life under the Tudors as a typical manor house and was added onto during the early part of the last century. Some sections are quite old, but I've managed to update a good part of it. Enough to keep everyone who stays in some degree of comfort at any rate."

"Ah," nodded Caroline wisely. "So the drains don't smell, then. That must be pleasant." Before Christopher could follow up on that rather provocative statement, she carried on. "And what about the grounds? Are they extensive?"

"They're certainly large enough to provide a good deal of employment, not just on the estate, but on the home farm and the four other farms that make up the bulk of the land. I have as much land under cultivation as I can manage without hurting the natural state of the environs too badly."

"No grand park sweeping into a panoramic horizon? No follies? No hermits?"

"There's plenty of room to go for a walk or a ride without trampling on the crops. Any place that age has seen its share of follies, I'm sure," Christopher said, deliberately misinterpreting her words. "And as for hermits, well I do spend a considerable amount of time there alone, Eleanor being much more enchanted with town life than I am, but at least I bathe semi-regularly and contrive to have my hair cut as frequently as my valet deems advisable."

"I expect it's never wise to disagree with the person who holds a razor to your throat every morning." Caroline's voice was solemn, but there was a twinkle in her eyes as she listened to Christopher's foolishness.

"It's one of the first precepts my father taught me," Christopher agreed. "And perhaps the most useful."

"He sounds like he was a practical man."

"Practical, yes." There was a bitter twist to Christopher's lip. "Sensible? That was something else entirely."

Caroline's curiosity was piqued. "Surely they're the same thing."

"On the contrary. A practical man loses twenty thousand pounds playing cards one night, and knowing that his reputation will receive considerable damage if he doesn't pay it off, something which on no account does he want to happen, mortgages his property in order to have the money to cover what was a completely useless and unnecessary expense. A sensible man recognizes that he shouldn't be gambling for such high stakes and doesn't incur the debt in the first place."

He spoke with a nonchalant air, as if the difference was purely academic, but Caroline had seen the way his lips tightened.

"Yes, I can see the distinction now," she said carefully. "Practicality is choosing a particular response to an event that may or may not have been one's own fault. Being sensible means not getting into a fix in the first place."

"Or responding in a way that doesn't make the whole situation worse," Christopher added.

"And how do you think I behaved, my lord, when I inserted myself into your conversation with that busybody at the inn when we first met? Practically or sensibly?"

"Can it be considered either practical or sensible for a young woman who is unmarried and unchaperoned to be travelling alone in the first place?" Christopher asked in response, delaying his own answer.

"Well, it wasn't my choice, but one must take circumstances into account. Perhaps it would have been more sensible to wait until Mrs. O'Donnell was able to travel before resuming my journey, but it wouldn't have been very kind. So I simply took all practical precautions. I believe your delineations of practical and sensible are a little less clear-cut than you'd have me believe. It was, perhaps, the practical thing to embark on this deception we have concocted, but no one would consider it sensible to allow myself to be completely under the power of an unmarried man with whom I had not the slightest acquaintanceship. Quite the contrary. Yet look how well it's turning out as we negotiate our way along this practical but nonsensical path."

****

Her words struck Christopher with the force of a cannon ball. Just the previous evening he had poured out his heart—or as much of it as any Englishman of good breeding was capable of—to Captain Waverly. After admitting him into his confidence about the sham marriage, he had confessed his growing attraction to the woman he was sheltering in his home. He told him how her voice had first cast a spell over him when he stumbled into her room that fateful night at the posting house; how her practical nature and willingness to work together to alleviate the situation rather than exacerbate things with a fit of hysteria had invoked his admiration.

How gradually, almost without noticing, he had fallen for her. His friend had agreed it was a deuced coil, and nodded wisely when Christopher had explained most forcefully that he could not under any circumstances take advantage of the situation. Despite Waverly's agreement, Christopher had continued to argue his case.

"To this day, I don't think she realizes that she could easily have forced me into a real marriage and no one would have thought she was doing anything that wasn't right and proper. But I don't think such a course of action ever occurred to her. And if it did she wouldn't have considered it either fair or...gentlemanly, for want of a better word. I can't possibly take advantage of that generosity of both spirit and action by going back on my word and seducing her under the very roof I had offered her as protection."

"No indeed." Waverly had poured out another large glass of claret for both of them and settled back into his chair. "What's to be done?"

"I'll just have to keep my distance," Christopher said bitterly, "and hope I continue to have the willpower to do so."

"No more waltzing then," Waverly suggested. "Damn good waltzer, Caroline is. Feels good in one's arms. Too much of that and you'd have danced her out on the balcony before the cat had time to lick its ear, and then where would you be?"

"I hadn't realized you'd made such a study of my wife's dancing prowess." There was ice coating the words.

"I like her," Waverly protested bravely. "Besides, she's not your wife, is she?"

"I'll thank you to keep your hands off her all the

same."

Recognizing that Christopher wasn't up to hearing the teasing under the words, his friend judiciously backed down.

"Didn't know she wasn't your wife when I danced with her, did I? Of course I'll keep my hands off her. Not my type anyway," he added to Christopher's stupefaction. "The question you haven't considered, though, is what *her* type is. Maybe it's you. How do you know she hasn't been struggling with the same attraction you're wrestling with?"

It was a question that kept Christopher up until the dawn started bringing a hint of gray to the sliver of night sky peeking through his bedroom window.

Chapter Thirteen

Now hearing Caroline's words, hearing the trust in her voice and the certainty that she would come to no harm under his care, he realized there was absolutely nothing he could do—would do—to betray that trust. If that meant never letting her know how he felt, well, it was a fair price to pay for having almost compromised her in the first place. If she did indeed feel the same way, and he wasn't vain enough to believe that she did, any closeness between them would only make the situation worse. He would be friendly. Even solicitous. But he would stop letting his guard down as he had just done when she threw that saucy smile in his direction as they raced across the turf. No matter how natural it felt. No matter how easy it was to both tease her and talk about the things that really mattered to him, the things that had formed his character and his precepts. The things that made him the man he was.

The things he had never ever shared with another soul.

So he forced a pleasant smile onto his lips and out of his eyes. "I stand corrected. Your admiral good sense has once again triumphed."

Caroline felt as though a bucket of cold water had been dashed into her face. One minute they were as comfortable together as the closest companions, the next she was being treated with the distant courtesy afforded the most encroaching mushrooms on the social scene. As though she were a cit who had dared to address a duke. The effrontery!

She managed to reply, though she didn't know what she said. She hoped she didn't make a fool of herself. She hoped she *hadn't* made a fool of herself. The fact of the matter was she occasionally forgot it was all a sham, that Christopher wasn't her husband in truth, that their companionable days would come to an end and any rapport she felt developing between them was only temporary.

Sometimes she deliberately allowed herself to forget. To pretend. She had obviously drifted too far into that fantasy, she suddenly realized, as his words and his withdrawal made it woefully, humiliatingly apparent, that Christopher had noticed the *tendre* she was developing for him. She steeled her spine. It wouldn't happen again.

"The morning is well along and I have some correspondence to answer. Shall we return?" she asked with all the cool politeness she could muster as she turned Princess back toward the bridle path and the safety of others.

It didn't take long for the *ton*, always watching and ever eager to comment, to remark on the fact that Lord and Lady Saxon had managed to get through the lovey-dovey honeymoon stage of their marriage with remarkable rapidity. Only a couple of weeks ago they'd practically been living in each other's pockets. It had verged on the disgraceful, some of the old tabbies had proclaimed. Now, when the newlyweds attended a ball, they danced with other partners as often as with each other, and it wasn't unusual for Lord Saxon to disappear into the card room before the supper dance had even been struck up. When they went riding or driving in the park, more and more frequently they were accompanied by Christopher's sister, and Christopher clearly no longer felt it incumbent upon him to accompany his bride to every musicale and salon she graced with her presence.

One rumor was put to rest in any case. The new Lady Saxon wasn't increasing. Only a monster would act that indifferently to a woman carrying the potential heir to Hawkings. Apparently, it had been a love match after all. Or at least, some of them noted, not a marriage of necessity. What kind of a marriage it was, they didn't presume to imagine. It was, after all, none of their business.

No matter what the marriage had now become.

Caroline began counting the days until the charade could be drawn to a conclusion, marking off a mental calendar as assiduously as she had imagined herself doing when she had faced the prospect of spending her days being trotted around society by her aunt's ancient crony. That, at least, was one pitfall she had managed to avoid. A carefully worded missive, worked out with the assistance of Christopher and his vaguely scandalized lawyer, had informed her erstwhile chaperone that she had managed to circumvent the strictures of the will and would not be spending the season under that good lady's aegis. Caroline took pains to thank her most prettily for her offered hospitality.

She had been dreading the possibility of running into her at one of the many social events she now routinely attended and was very relieved to discover that the lady, contrary to how she had presented herself to her old school friend, was not such a fixture of society after all. Without Caroline to escort around and the accompanying income to supplement the widow's small jointure that the addition to her household would have afforded her—as well as what she might have skimmed from dressmakers and milliners for providing such good custom, she retired to the less taxing and less expensive haven of her second son's manse and spent the season terrorizing her daughter-in-law, her grandchildren, and as many of the local people she could waylay on their way to seek their minister's counsel.

Eleanor, who had naturally been amongst the first to notice the increasing coolness between her brother and his make-believe wife, at first said nothing. But as the easy comradery that had grown up between the three of them continued to dissipate, at least between Caroline and Christopher, she ventured some gentle questioning. It didn't go well.

Caroline, whom she approached first in a woman-to-woman kind of way and with the absolute conviction that her brother was, of course, to blame for the estrangement, was both cool and unresponsive.

"Eleanor, you make it sound as if we've had some sort of lover's quarrel," she said in response to a gently worded question, her voice unaffected and carefully amused. "You know, sometimes I think you forget we aren't actually married."

Eleanor persisted. "Of course I don't forget, but the fact of the matter is you and Christopher used to be quite comfortable in each other's company, and now if one of you walks into a room the other will almost certainly leave it within a minute or two."

"Well, we've accomplished what we initially set out to do," Caroline countered. "Society is convinced we have a real marriage. No one will question its legitimacy now. We can let our guard down a bit. You can hardly expect Christopher to continue dancing attendance on me at the rate he was forced to in the beginning. What a trial that would be for the poor man."

Clearly, there would be no confidences coming from Caroline and her words only served to convince Eleanor that Christopher was, indeed, to blame for the coolness that had grown between them. Confronting her brother, however, gained her no greater understanding than her conversation with Caroline had done.

"I really don't see what you're on about," were his terse words. "Has Caroline been complaining about my treatment of her?" They were in the withdrawing salon and he paused in the rearrangement of the invitations on the mantel to shoot her an accusatory look beneath drawn black brows.

"Of course not!"

"Then I fail to understand the point of this rather tedious inquisition. I'm sure Caroline was finding the constant company of a comparative stranger as taxing as I was. I dare say she's quite relieved to get a bit of peace and quiet away from my assiduous attendance."

Eleanor had her own ideas about how relieved Caroline would be under such circumstances and they aligned very well with her views on Christopher's feelings in the matter. However, she had known Christopher his entire life and she recognized that tone. Clearly there was no point in raising that particular subject. She allowed herself to make a cool observation of her own.

"I don't know how Caroline feels. I'm not in her confidence. And over the years I've generally found that it's very difficult to know how someone feels if you're afraid to ask them. Don't you agree?" she asked, her eyes wide and innocent.

"No, deuce take it, I don't," Christopher replied and flung himself out of the room. It was most uncharacteristic behavior. Eleanor, who had become quite fond of her pseudo-sister-in-law, allowed herself a satisfied smile at his retreating back.

Caroline was finding the coolness between herself and Christopher both taxing and a great relief. Lying alone in her bed at night, she forced herself to admit that her feelings for him were warmer than they had any right to be. She had grown up in virtual isolation from her own class and knew little about the society he moved through with such style and ease. Nonetheless, she was under no illusion that it was his newness that attracted her. Since coming to London she had been introduced to many men—young ones, old ones, handsome ones, rich ones and ones who were renowned for their singular charm and polished address. None of them could hold a candle to Lord Saxon, who had a way of making her heart flutter simply by strolling into a room and gracing her with his characteristic half smile, the one that barely moved his lips but lit up his eyes like sunshine on amber.

His cool courtesy, which she returned with head held high and indifferent voice, was close to torture after weeks of feeling the warmth of his hand on her back as he escorted her across a room or the way he leaned toward her intently when she spoke. She had grown accustomed to his attentions. More. She had learned to bask in them.

It was very impractical and as far as she could tell, that didn't matter. It simply couldn't be helped and that's all there was to it.

The withdrawal of those attentions had hurt. There was no way Caroline could deny it. And when she was being particularly honest with herself, she also admitted to a feeling of humiliation. She wasn't versed in the ways of the world. She was too practical, too inexperienced in hiding her thoughts and feelings. There had never been any need to do so when rollicking in the countryside of another land. So, she must have given herself away. Christopher must have seen her growing…affection, for want of a better word, and realizing the damage it could do, had cut her off before it could get any worse. It had been for her own good and she should be grateful he had handled things so diplomatically. She tried to tell herself it was better this way; she insisted to herself that the inevitable separation would be all the more bearable if their increasing closeness was halted before it did any more damage, regardless of what Christopher's motivation had been. That she should not just accept Christopher's wisdom in withdrawing his attentions, but be grateful for it.

But such thoughts only worked in the daytime. Lying in bed alone under the cold moon's gaze, all she wanted was to feel Christopher's lips on hers, his arms around her, his eyes blazing and his words those of love. Just once. No matter the consequences. No matter how miserable she felt afterwards.

Just once.

Chapter Fourteen

The Duchess of Chatterton's grand ball was considered one of *the* social events of the season. It wasn't even a case of everyone who was anyone attending. There were plenty of people quite convinced they fell comfortably within that select group, but whose invitation, they forced themselves to assume, had somehow been mislaid. As the duchess herself was fond of saying, cream always rose to the top and she was not prepared to invite anyone who would ever do less than effortlessly float around the dance floor. Behavior counted as much as breeding. There was a certain marquis who still, twenty years later, was left firmly off the invitation list for, under the influence of too much of the duke's excellent claret, once propositioning a young debutante as shy as she was shocked by his slurred and improper words.

When an invitation was extended to Lord and Lady Saxon, Eleanor waved it around the drawing room as though it were a personal victory and tribute to her own successful launching of Caroline into society.

"Must we go?" Caroline asked when informed of the treat in store.

Eleanor was aghast. "Must?" she exclaimed. "Do you know how difficult it is to earn one of these cartes? I haven't been invited to darken the ballroom doorway since I had the temerity to allow myself to be widowed ten years ago. Quite frankly, I'm not sure how you and Christopher managed it unless Mrs. Winthrop put in a good word for you. She and the duchess have been bosom buddies since they stowed away on the ark together."

It was a continued source of mystery to Eleanor the way that elderly lady had taken a shine to Caroline. It was even more of a mystery the way Caroline seemed to esteem the old harridan back.

"Perhaps implying that the duchess is as old as Noah has something to do with your lack of an invitation," Caroline suggested.

"Nonsense. She's just extremely ornery. I shall enjoy the opportunity to stay home and read a good book."

"You'll do no such thing," was Caroline's immediate respond. "If I know anything about it, you'll attend the Hampton's ball instead, so you can see who else wasn't invited to the Chatterton's and make yourself feel better about the infinitely more amusing company you're keeping."

Eleanor laughed. "In an earlier age you'd have been burned as a witch. That is exactly what I'll do, just like everyone else trying to pretend they were only snubbed by accident and are quietly relieved they don't have to go to the trouble of turning down an invitation they had no intention of accepting in the first place."

"I wish I could join you," Caroline admitted. "I feel no great desire to attend a ball half my friends and acquaintances have been excluded from."

"Don't be absurd. After almost two months of socializing you'll know practically everyone there, and you'll be surprised at what a lot of them you'll enjoy seeing. There's a reason her invitations are so coveted. You go and have a good time. After all, the season is almost over. Go out with a bang."

Caroline had no intention of doing any such thing, but when she looked at herself in the mirror after allowing Andrews *carte blanche* with her hair and choice of accessories, she felt as fine again as she had on that evening so many weeks ago when Christopher had stood at the bottom of the stairs looking up at her and, she had felt in her bones, seen someone who bore little resemblance to the ever practical Miss Saxon he so carelessly teased.

The dress was a deep silken sapphire that shimmered as she moved as though she herself was lit from within. The neckline was much more modest than the more dashing members of the *ton* were wont to wear, but it hinted beguilingly at decadence and the possibility of slipping past its seemingly inadequate anchorage. Andrews had been ruthless with the laces of Caroline's stays and her waist had never seemed tinier, although she had stopped short at allowing them to be pulled so tight that breathing could only be done with difficulty, and eating and drinking not at all. The way the gown clung to her hips convinced Caroline that even were she still here, the chances of being invited to next year's ball would be seriously in question. If the duchess caught a glimpse of the polish Andrews had daringly applied to her toenails, she was sure the chances would drop to nil.

She couldn't wait for Christopher to see them.

****

The first thing Christopher noticed as Caroline descended the stairs toward him were her toes in the open silver slippers she wore on her feet.

Their nails were red. Really red. The kind of red that would have driven Cleopatra Nile green with envy. The kind of red that kept sane men from their sleep at night.

As the toes got closer, Christopher forced himself to look higher. He immediately recognized his mistake.

He hadn't thought Caroline knew how to undulate. That was a misconception on his part. He wrenched his gaze higher.

Dear God, her *décolletage*. How did that dress stay up? Newton's laws be damned. Gravity had just been given its walking papers.

"Good evening, Christopher," Caroline said coolly. "I'm sorry. Have I been keeping you waiting?"

In an attempt to breathe and talk at the same time while maintaining eye contact, Christopher's voice came out like stone. "Not at all." He cleared this throat and tried again. "You look very fine," he managed.

"Indeed?" Was that a fleeting glimpse of disappointment in her eyes? He couldn't be sure. "Then we make a fine couple. For you, too, look very…fine." She held one gloved hand out for him to take. "I assume you have the carriage waiting and since Eleanor won't be joining us, we can leave at once if that suits you."

Caroline wrapped up in a cloak and hidden by the darkness of the carriage's interior was exactly what Christopher needed. "Of course," he said, immediately, his voice still strained. "Although I was prepared to wait much longer, I had the horses brought round just in case. We shall set a new fashion for making an early arrival."

Caroline raised her eyebrows half an inch, and

looked at him sideways from under darkened lashes. "Oh dear. Do I look as though I've rushed my preparation?"

"Not at all!" It was in near panic that he wondered what more she could possibly do to make herself look any better than she already did. "I just…" he trailed off, realizing anything he said would somehow end up making the whole situation worse. "You look…"

"Fine. Yes, I know. Shall we be off?"

He followed her to the door meekly, hoping his equilibrium returned before he made a complete cake of himself in front of half of London.

While certainly not the first guests to arrive, Lord and Lady Saxon were there early enough to be greeted in a less hurried manner than those who arrived later would receive.

"I'm so pleased you were able to come. I'm very glad to see you both," the duchess said graciously before directing her regal eye in Christopher's direction. "I'm happy to see you settled finally, Saxon. It's past time you came back and took up your responsibilities again."

"I'm sure you are right, Your Grace." Christopher raised her hand to his lips and bowed low before continuing. "You're certainly not the first one to tell me so. I'm even starting to believe it myself. In fact, I'll be leaving for Hawkings quite soon and I daresay my steward will throw himself on my neck in gratitude."

He was annoyed to notice that the duchess, who hadn't reached her preeminent position in society on rank alone, hadn't missed the startled look Caroline had thrown in his direction and then quickly supressed.

"I hope you don't mean to suggest you'll be

leaving your lovely bride alone here," she said.

"Not at all," he replied smoothly. "Where I go Caroline will, of course, accompany me."

"Of course," Caroline agreed. "As we discussed. I just hadn't realized the time had passed so quickly and our departure was so imminent."

"Well, enjoy your solitude there together. Chatterton and I have very fond memories of our time on his estates before the children were born." She turned to the next guests, who had been waiting patiently for their turn to be greeted.

It was a relief to see that Captain Waverly was also amongst the early arrivals. He came over to them as soon as they appeared, cutting a dash through the gathering in his scarlet dress regimentals.

"Good Lord," Christopher exclaimed when he reached them. "I thought this was meant to be some sort of exclusive event."

"Evidently not, since you somehow managed to wangle an invitation," Waverly grinned, not at all put out by the less than enthusiastic welcome. "Lady Saxon," he said, turning toward Caroline and bowing over her hand with a twinkle in his eye. "I assume the invitation was yours and they let this reprobate in because you wanted an escort."

Caroline laughed and Christopher couldn't help but notice it was the first time he had heard her do so in many days.

"You know I could never admit to such a thing, even if it were true."

"Which it isn't," Christopher interjected. "I'd forgotten you were related to Lady Chatterton through some suspect twists of the genealogical tree. That explains what you're doing here at any event. We, of course, were invited on our own merit."

"Yes, she's my mother's godmother. But to be fair, it didn't do Charlie any good," Waverly said, referring to his younger brother. "She's taken him in dislike for some unfathomable reason, and he's languishing elsewhere."

Christopher, who had known Charles Waverly almost as long as he'd known Robert, and had no illusions about his devil-may-care approach to life, wasn't surprised he hadn't received an invitation and would have been very surprised indeed to learn he had been left languishing as a result. Quite the contrary.

"I expect she only invited you because she has set herself a quota of red uniforms to decorate the ballroom. If you'd have enlisted in the Rifle Brigade you'd have been languishing with Charlie."

"Well since I had the forethought to choose the Coldstream rather than the bad taste to allow myself to be uniformed in bottle green of all things, I wonder if I can prevail upon you, Lady Saxon, to save the second waltz for me. I'm already committed for the first one, I'm afraid."

Caroline was happy to oblige and the three chatted together comfortably for a few minutes before Waverly left to claim a dance with one of the nervous debutantes starting to array themselves along the edges of the ballroom.

"Shall we dance?" Christopher asked, holding out his arm. "I'm sure Robert is only the first of many to ask, and if I don't claim a dance now, I won't get the opportunity later."

Caroline hesitated before replying. "If you wish,"

Barbara Burke

she finally said. "There's no need if you prefer not."

"Don't be ridiculous. Why would I prefer not to dance with the most beautiful woman in the room?"

Caroline's startled blue eyes, which had been surveying the room, flew up to meet his own. "Beautiful? Now who's being ridiculous? You've never called me that before."

"A mistake on my part. Shall we?" He held out his arm.

By the time Captain Waverly came to claim his dance, the room had filled up nicely and Caroline had danced twice with Christopher as well as with two other men she had gotten to know since arriving in London. The first was a shy bachelor who had learned he could let his guard down a bit with the plain-spoken and already taken—he believed—Irishwoman, and the second a bluff widower who liked the fact that he didn't have to do the pretty with Saxon's new wife, and could spend the time discussing possible candidates to replace the late and largely unlamented mother of his seven clamorous and increasingly tiresome children.

As it had filled, the room had become increasingly stuffy, and after a few whirls around the dance floor, Waverly, noticing the pink tinge to Caroline's usual ivory complexion, suggested they stroll out onto the terrace for a breath of fresh air.

"For though it's not the crush it could be, it's still hot enough to wilt the starchiest collars and I think Christopher, who I see has completely disappeared from view, cannot object to me doing my best to revive your spirits."

Caroline laughed a trifle bitterly as she accompanied him through one of the long doors that

162

lined the room. "I admit it's become quite warm, but am I really so transparent that you can see my spirits as well as my energy are in need of revitalizing?"

"Now how would you like me to answer that?" he asked gently as he guided her across the marble flagstones toward the rail where they could look across the lamp lit gardens. "I could say you were incapable of exhibiting a single flaw, which would in no way be a complete rasper, or I could gently suggest you and Christopher have been having the devil of a time of it and are starting to fray at the edges."

Caroline laughed nervously. "How on earth do you expect me to respond to such a statement?"

"Well, honesty mostly works best when saving face and feelings aren't involved. Perhaps it would help if I told you that Christopher and I are very close friends and have become over the years quite used to taking each other into our confidence."

"So you're aware of our situation?" Caroline asked quietly. "Christopher hadn't told me. I wonder who else he's seen fit to inform."

"I don't think he meant to tell me. He just needed to talk one night, and I can't believe he's said a word to anyone else. I assure you, as he knows himself, it will go no farther."

"Thank you. In some ways it's a relief to have another person in on our secret. We've been walking on tenterhooks every time we stick our noses outside the door in case we say or do something to raise suspicion."

Major Waverly glanced around the terrace. Though they were standing apart, other couples had stepped outside to take advantage of the cooler air. The possibility they could be interrupted or, worse, overheard, could not be discounted. "Why don't we take a small walk through the shrubbery and you can give me your version of events."

"The one in which Christopher doesn't appear as quite such a villain?"

"Ah, I see you're getting to know my friend very well," Waverly laughed as he escorted her down the short flight of stone stairs to the darker confines of the garden below. "That's exactly the story I'm eager to hear."

Chapter Fifteen

"It's a shame Mrs. Westmore couldn't have joined us," Andrews said brightly from her position on the back-facing seat in Christopher's elegant travelling carriage. "She must think of Hawkings as her home, having been brought up there and all."

"Certainly more than mine," Caroline agreed from the facing seat. "How odd it must be to arrive for the first time at a house that's been in the family for centuries and immediately take over running the entire household."

"But that's what you're born to do, my lady. There's nothing odd about it."

"Not I," Caroline responded firmly. "Very soon I'll be back in the home I was raised in, and it seems very unlikely I'll leave it for this long a time ever again."

"I wouldn't say that if I were you," Andrews warned. "It's not up to us mere mortals to understand the turns and twists of fate. You no more know where life will lead you than the horses pulling this carriage know where they're going. And that's a fact there's no denying, my lady."

"Well, maybe you are right," Caroline conceded. "But I do know Eleanor would much rather stay in London than visit her ancestral acres. Perhaps when one is truly married and knows one will never return, one loses one's attachment to the home of one's childhood.

And that's a very good thing now that I think about it. We can't have half the population pining for a home they can never return to."

"Indeed, my lady. That would be a pickle and no mistake."

"I think it's time you stopped calling me 'my lady', don't you? The masquerade is drawing to an end and we will soon all be taking off our disguises and going back to normal life."

"But that's how I think of you, my lady. I can't change now. Besides, it would look odd if I suddenly started referring to you as 'miss'."

It occurred to Caroline for the first time, though she was ashamed to admit it even to herself, that Andrews' life had been turned upside down as much as her own.

"What is to become of you when this is all over, Jane?" she asked. "Will you have to go back to being a regular upstairs maid again? That hardly seems fair. I don't suppose you'd like to give up your position in the Saxon household. Otherwise I could give you a reference."

Andrews shifted uncomfortably and her rosy complexion took on an ever deeper red hue.

"Oh no, my lady. Townsend's got it all worked out. She thinks she can put in a good word for me with one or two families she knows of with young daughters on the verge of coming out. She thinks I should be able to get something without much difficulty at all. It won't be the same as having the dressing of you, of course, but I'm sure I'll get on fine and be able to move up if I work hard and don't send a ginger out in an orange dress and no freckle cream on her face."

"Goodness, that would be a catastrophe!" Caroline's deep-throated laugh rang out. "But meaning no offence to your indomitable mentor, wouldn't a reference from me go farther than one from Townsend?"

"But, my lady…" Andrews squirmed again. "…You'll be dead. Or at least that's what everyone's supposed to think. How could you write me a reference?"

Caroline stared blankly for a minute as the carriage continued its rumble along the irregular road. "I'm afraid I'd rather forgotten that part of the arrangement. People are truly going to think I've died, aren't they?"

To some her supposed death would be a piece of gossip to wonder over and then forget as the next *on dit* clamoured for attention. But not to everyone. She thought of old Mrs. Winthrop of whom she had become so fond, of Lady Robinson, who she had learned to rely on almost as much as Eleanor to see her through the shoals of society, and a host of others she had danced, dined and driven with. Some of them would mourn her; perhaps not for long, but with sincerity nonetheless. It was an aspect of the situation, like Andrews' disrupted career path, she had not given a thought to before this moment. She began to wonder if she was the most selfish person alive—quite an accomplishment given all the frivolous creatures she had met during her two months' sojourn amongst the upper echelons of society.

"Well, of course they will, or the whole thing will have been for naught," Andrews replied. "I expect Lord Saxon will go away again so he doesn't have to go into mourning and receive everyone's condolences."

Another aspect of the situation Caroline hadn't

considered. She knew how much Christopher had been looking forward to settling down to managing his estate and carrying out his duties in London. Perhaps he had even been considering marriage. He might have already had someone in mind—someone who might no longer be available when his period of mourning was finally over. She would happily return to her own small, restricted world and carry on with her plans without a care or a backward glance. Or at least she firmly told herself that would be the case. But he would spend a year, maybe two or more, continuing to pick up the pieces from the fallout of that one ruinous mistake. Either pretending to mourn a woman who had never really existed or living in exile until that same creature of fantasy had mainly been forgotten.

It almost seemed as if they should have been married in truth. At least that way they'd be paying an equal price.

Even if it made them both miserable.

It was at that rather depressing point that the object of her ruminations, who had been riding alongside the carriage on his own horse, stuck his head in the window. She realized they had come to a halt.

"We're almost there," he said. "But if you'd like to stretch your legs, there's a good view of the house from this vantage point. May I escort you for a short walk?"

Caroline realized how stiff she had become after two days of almost constant travel cooped up in the small compartment, no matter how luxurious it was compared to other forms of transport. All thoughts of the future forgotten, she readily descended from the carriage and accompanied him up a short path through the trees off the main road.

Before long they came out onto a verge that looked out across a valley with a small river meandering along the bottom. The land rose gradually on the other side and tucked into the gentle hill could be seen a mellow brick building surrounded on three sides by park land and trees. A dappled light danced shadows across its high, smooth walls.

"Hawkings is beautiful," Caroline said simply.

"Yes," Christopher agreed without further comment.

They stood silently for a minute, and though the vista was striking, Caroline felt herself growing increasingly uncomfortable. She couldn't forget the revelations and realizations the conversation with her maid had evoked.

"Christopher, I'm so sorry," she said finally. "When we began this whole silly charade I didn't think about anything except overcoming the immediate problem as painlessly as possible. But now we're stuck with this monster we've created, and you're the one who will be forced to bear the brunt of it."

He turned to her, startled, his dark brows drawing together sharply. "What on earth are you talking about?"

"Andrews explained to me, or rather brought me to realize, what a trying time you are still facing. Here I was thinking I'd just go back to Ireland and all would be well."

"And that's the case," he interrupted.

"But not for you it isn't. First you've been forced to assume the guise of a married man and now you'll be forced to play the widower. How much longer will you have to put your life on hold because of one night's mistake?"

His brow cleared and he answered in a mild tone. "There are many people in the world, possibly a great many more than we realize, who have their whole life permanently altered as a result of one night's indiscretion. A set period of time with a clear end date doesn't seem too much to pay. Rather like a jail term, when you think about it. Once it's done, you're free and clear."

Caroline ignored his attempt at levity as worthy of neither consideration nor response. "But it's not fair! This situation is as much my fault as yours."

"Fair? Is this my practical Miss Saxon I hear talking about 'fair'? Fair has nothing to do with the way life unfolds, and who would want it to? It sounds dashed dull."

"Don't talk foolishness, my lord. You know exactly what I mean. Why should your life be so disrupted when mine will continue on as before?"

Christopher's face grew serious and his dark gaze focused fully on her. There was no teasing sound in his voice as he spoke. "I agree life would be simpler without the charade. And, in fact, I have a plan in place that I hope will preclude any draconic sacrifices." He stepped closer until their bodies were only a breath apart. "But even so, perhaps living discomfited for a year or so is a price worth paying for the privilege of having known you for the last two months."

Caroline's mouth actually dropped open at his words. She couldn't think of a thing to say that wouldn't sound as if she…as though she…like she'd completely misinterpreted the meaning behind his words.

Because he couldn't have meant what it sounded like he meant. Could he? He couldn't have.

She closed her mouth firmly and tried to think of some intelligent way to respond to his words—some way of answering that wouldn't make her out to be a complete fool when he realized what she had allowed her crazed imagination to believe, even for a moment. As she furiously thought, a drop of water hit her squarely on the tip of her nose. She took her cue gratefully.

"I believe it is starting to rain, my lord. Shall we return to the carriage?"

By the time they reached Hawkings, some half an hour later, the rain was falling quite steadily. Caroline was rushed through the door and up to her room before she had much of a chance to take in her surroundings. It was with considerable interest, therefore, that she looked around her after being freshened up and making her way down the stairs to where Christopher waited for her in a small salon. It was also with considerably more aplomb than she had been able to muster earlier.

After accepting a glass of sherry and arranging herself on the small settee close to the fire she spoke in calm measured tones. "You mentioned you had a plan for the future, my lord. Can you tell me what it is?"

Christopher studied her for a moment without answering. She was dressed plainly but elegantly, her shoulders enveloped in a navy Cashmere shawl over a quiet blue dress. Her hair was dressed simply, pulled back from her face with three small ringlets silently drawing attention to the delicate pink tips of her earlobes and the creamy length of her throat. It continued to amaze him that she didn't know she was beautiful.

But her beauty, though it had on more than one occasion interfered with his ability to breathe properly, was such a small part of what made her Caroline that he wasn't sure it even mattered. With some women, their beauty was the only thing of significance about them, the only quality they themselves and society as a whole paid any attention to or considered of value, and when it was gone, as it inevitably would be, there was very little left of worth about them at all. With her it was almost incidental. When she was ninety she would be as beguiling as she was now.

"I don't think I will," he responded lightly. "There's no certainty to it and I'd rather not spoil things by speaking prematurely. I've managed to arrange your travel requirements and you should be able to set out in a couple of days. We just have to make sure the coachman has been given enough time to visit his daughter and new grandson, or he'll be driving hell for leather the entire way in order to get back all the sooner."

It was a deliberate change in subject, but Caroline accepted it with equanimity. If Christopher chose not to speak there was no means or method she was aware of to make him.

"It seems something of a shame we came to Hawkings at all," Caroline said. "I'm very glad to have seen it after all you've told me, but it has complicated matters somewhat, trying to organize which servants would be where and how we were going to smuggle me away. Perhaps it would have been better had I just headed straight home."

"That would never have done. That parade through

the village at the height of day wasn't an accident, you know. It's vital as many as possible of the townspeople see you so they can attest to your presence here if anyone starts asking questions later. You can't just disappear completely."

Caroline wasn't entirely sure she accepted the logic of his contention. But she had done some long, hard thinking and had realized she was willing to accept Christopher's arrangements just so she could see him in these surroundings and remember him here when memory became the only thing she had left of these stolen days.

"I'm sure you know best." She contented herself with replying and drew a bark of laughter.

"I wish Eleanor could hear you say that," Christopher said. "I don't believe I've ever been credited with knowing best before. In fact, I'm not at all sure this isn't the first time you've ever said such a thing."

"I'm sure you are wrong, my lord—"

"That's more like it!"

Caroline chose to ignore his interjection, though the look she cast him was militant. "You are, *generally speaking*, a sensible man. I must have commented on it in the past. If I have not done so, then I apologize for it now. It was ill done."

"Caroline, you have completely taken the wind out of my sails. It's dashed unfair. How am I to maintain my righteous indignation in the face of your unwavering good sense and fair mindedness?"

"You cannot," was the prompt reply. "Now tell me about your plans for Hawkings. You have mentioned several times that there are alterations and improvements you wish to carry on with. Now that I have seen something of the place, I can more easily envision what you mean."

Christopher was always happy to discuss his projects and listened attentively to Caroline's suggestions when she tentatively broached them. The evening passed pleasantly enough, and when the candles started guttering in their holders, it was with something of a shock that they realized the lateness of the hour.

"If you're up for a ride in the morning, I can take you out to the south reach and show you exactly what I have in mind," Christopher suggested, rising from where he had been sitting in the brocaded chair across from Caroline. "But in the meantime, I suggest we retire before we're left in the dark. I had no idea how late it was becoming."

"Nor I," admitted Caroline, standing up and brushing her skirts into order. "Andrews will be wondering what has become of me. I hope you can promise me a good long gallop tomorrow. I need to shake off the *ennui* that my comfortable, but nonetheless, confining carriage ride has induced, especially since I face another in just a couple of days."

"I'm quite sure something can be arranged." There was a twinkle in Christopher's eye as they climbed the stairs to their rooms. "Wear stout gloves and boots."

Caroline took his advice, and the next morning saw her clad in a stylish, but practical riding habit that would stand up to the kind of hell-for-leather romp that would have had the doyens of Hyde Park swooning in their carriages had anyone dared to ride in such a manner within its august and restricted confines. They set forth immediately after breakfast. Christopher knew enough by now to ensure the head groom didn't send up a horse "suitable for a lady," and Caroline almost grinned when she saw the sleek bay gelding dancing beside Christopher's horse.

"Aren't you the beautiful laddy now?" she crooned as she approached, voice gentle and hand held out for inspection.

"Do you know you always get much more Irish as soon as you've got a horse in your general environs?" Christopher asked with some amusement.

"Well I am Irish, and it's the Irish in me that loves the creatures so much."

The bay whickered gently into her hand and she brought the other one up to scratch his forelock. He turned his head toward her.

"Yes, I know, you're after slobbering down my front and getting me in trouble with my maid, aren't you?" she asked, in a tone of voice that suggested she heartily approved of such a course of action. "But we mustn't upset her, so I'll thank you to look elsewhere for something to slaver all over." She walked around to the horse's left side, and accepting a boost from Christopher, settled into the saddle. She gave the horse's neck a smack of appreciation and rubbed along the side of his mane, causing him to arch his neck and blow softly through his lips. "Now let's see if you move as prettily as you flirt with your rider."

It was a beautiful morning, and they soon left the immediate surroundings of the house behind. Christopher showed Caroline the site of the improvements they had discussed the evening before, and there was, indeed, a long ridge ideally suited to riding as though they were a pair of English spies with Napoleon's entire army at their heels.

Throughout the morning, Christopher was as polite and attentive as anyone could wish. He was all that was pleasant and Caroline wanted to scream in frustration. She would leave in a few days, perhaps never to see him again. Probably never to see him again, because how could she do so? She remembered the warmth of his touch on other rides. She remembered the warmth in his eyes when he'd looked at her. She had hoped for a crack in his armor, but he remained a perfect gentleman.

She was finally forced to conclude that, despite the way he had sometimes looked at her, she was mistaken. There was no crack in his armor because he wasn't wearing any. He didn't need to protect himself against her. She meant nothing to him. She spent the rest of the day, as she spent the rest of the week, as they dined and as they walked through the house and the grounds and as he introduced her to the rather overpowering denizens of the gloomy portrait gallery, telling herself what a good thing that was. How much better it would be to leave with no regrets. With no memories of might have beens to keep her awake at night when she was back where she belonged under her own roof. It would make him so much easier to forget. She told herself so over and over again.

It didn't help.

And still Christopher smiled and conversed and kept his distance.

Chapter Sixteen

It had been a full week since Caroline had left, since Christopher had managed to hand her into the carriage without grasping her hand. Since he'd let her go. He'd spent the intervening days being busier than he ever remembered being in his life before. After years of careful investment and strategic improvements to increase revenues, the renovations and repairs he had envisioned for so long were now within his grasp. There was much to be done and he was eager to begin.

He spent days in the saddle, inspecting, making sure his ideas were workable, discussing every aspect with his estate manager, ensuring the man's cooperation for when he wasn't there. The evenings were spent pouring over plans and reading about the latest developments in agriculture. He found it all fascinating.

He found it all lonely. He wanted to discuss his ideas with Caroline, to listen to her opinion on whatever he was working on. He wanted to watch her tilt her head that certain way she had when she was considering the pros and cons of a particular proposition. He wanted to hear her ideas and consider the pros and cons of her propositions—he was sure she would have plenty. He wanted her companionship and her partnership. His manager and a bottle of port, though both of inestimable value in their own ways, made poor substitutions for her whiskey-soaked voice and gentle hands. But he'd quickly learned that everything and everyone did.

With thunder threatening, he'd decided to ride back to the house in the middle of the afternoon and perhaps look at some of the interior repairs and updates that needed doing and which he had been avoiding. The sight of a carriage just pulling up to the front door caused him to pull his horse up sharply some small distance away. He didn't recognize the equipage, except to notice that it bore no coat of arms. It must be a member of the local gentry. They'd—he'd—been lucky so far and allowed to enjoy an unprecedented degree of solitude, although he suspected luck had received a nudge from the servants he had brought with him. A general suggestion dropped in certain ears in the village would ensure that no one would impose themselves upon the lord and lady of the manor until the lord and lady were ready to accept guests.

Clearly this person or persons, whoever it was, hadn't gotten the message. He debated whether or not to turn tail and risk the coming storm before sighing and continuing on to the house. He was in no mood to entertain, but he wasn't prepared to risk a wetting to avoid it. That seemed to somehow verge on the cowardly. Besides, he'd be in for a proper trimming from the head groom if he allowed his horse's leathers to get wet.

He arrived at the foot of the stairs leading up to the entrance just as his visitors—there were two of them, he now saw—were approaching the front door to knock. The sound of his horse's hooves on the gravel caused the unwelcome guests to turn toward him and his heart sank. Standing before him was the very picture of contented English gentry folk. The man, his waistcoat and jacket already stretched over an ever-widening girth doffed a low styled beaver hat and bowed rather uncomfortably toward Christopher. His expression was half resignation and half discomfort. The woman on his arm, smiling determinedly through guinea curls from under the latest fashionable bonnet, had a certain predatory gleam in her bright blue eyes. Christopher rather thought a lion might cast such a speculative glance over an unsuspecting gazelle. His heart dropped still further when he realized who it was.

Though it had been more than two months since they'd first encountered each other, he recognized the gentleman immediately. It was the busybody from the Hare and Hounds, the inn where he had first met Caroline, the one whose interference had been responsible for everything that had happened since. Not knowing whether to draw his cork or shake his hand Christopher swung off his horse with practised ease and stood, holding the reins tightly in one hand. He felt at a decided disadvantage standing at the bottom of his own stairs, and wished a stable boy would miraculously appear to take his horse away and relieve him of the discomfort of feeling like an interloper on his own doorstep.

"Saxon!" the woman cried in what she no doubt considered a melodious trill. She let go of her companion's arm and hurried down the steps toward him, holding out both hands. "How lovely to see you again."

He held out the hand that wasn't holding on to the reins and bowed politely. "Miss Winthr..." he stopped. "Excuse me, Winthrop is no longer appropriate, is it?

I'm afraid I've forgotten your married name." He wasn't sure if he'd ever heard it. One of the small mercies of the recent situation he and Caroline had been forced to endure was that Annabelle Winthrop's older sister and her meddlesome new husband had not come to town for the season.

She trilled again. There was no other way to describe it. "It's Winterbottom. Isn't it too ridiculous? However, what can one do? A name is still a rose or some such nonsense. Isn't that correct? But you've met my dear Winterbottom, haven't you?" She gestured imperiously and her husband, who had been watching her with resigned apprehension, came down the stairs.

"Well I've certainly encountered your husband, although I didn't know it was he at the time," Christopher answered smoothly and drew his hand gently out of her grasp. "I'm not sure 'met' is quite the right word." He turned toward the gentleman. "How do you do, uh, Mr. Winterbottom, is it?"

"That's right, my lord. Plain Mister is good enough for me." He shook hands with a surprisingly firm grasp. "I hope you don't mind us calling. Clarissa seemed to feel there could be no objection since your families have been neighbours pretty much since the conquest. I've just bought a place nearby so she can be close to her childhood home whenever she wishes."

Christopher was at a loss to respond and very nearly blurted out an objection. He was saved when the massive door opened and the butler stepped outside and bowed formally.

"My lord," he said. "I've sent someone to fetch a boy for the horse. He should be along momentarily. In the meantime, unorthodox though it may be, perhaps you would allow me to hold the creature while you escort your guests inside. Tea will be served in the main drawing room shortly."

"Ah, Branston." Christopher tried to keep the relief out of his voice. "Splendid idea." He handed the reins over gratefully.

"How lovely," Mrs. Winterbottom exclaimed, taking Christopher's arm. "I can't wait to meet Lady Saxon. Annabelle has told me all about her."

"Oh." Christopher stopped halfway up the stairs. "I'm afraid that isn't possible. Caroline is indisposed. I don't believe she's left her rooms these three days past, and I'm sure she won't be coming down today. What do you think, Branston?"

"Indeed, my lord. I do not believe there is any hope of us seeing her ladyship this afternoon," was the bland response.

Winterbottom looked anxious. "Perhaps we should postpone our visit, my love," he suggested. "Not really the thing when the lady of the house isn't well."

She stood indecisively, petulance forming into familiar lines on her face. "How vexing. We've come all this way. But I suppose you're right. It wouldn't really be the thing to visit when the lady of the house is unable to receive us. But we'll come back next week! I'm sure she'll be better by then, won't she, Christopher?"

He was at a loss to answer her. "I certainly hope she'll be in the best of health. But I'm not sure what our plans are. I really dare not make any without consulting her."

Clarissa laughed. "Oh, I'm sure she'll be pining for a fresh face by then. After all, the honeymoon's long over and there's terribly little to do in the country." She tripped merrily back to the waiting carriage, all peevishness forgotten, and held out her hand as Christopher opened the door. "Until then," she said and climbed inside.

"Er, nice to meet you properly, Saxon," her husband contributed, before adding his bulk to the interior of the carriage. "Good day."

Christopher, hands on hips, and Branston, rigidly upright, stood and watched as the carriage made its way down the long drive to the road.

"Branston, you rogue. 'No hope of seeing her ladyship this afternoon' indeed. Let's hope the fat's not in the fire. I may have to dash for the continent again."

"Sufficient unto the day is the evil thereof, my lord."

Christopher glanced at the butler sharply. "If you've taken to quoting scripture then we're in a deeper mess than I thought. You leave me feeling strangely uncomforted. Here comes the boy finally. Let's away inside before the threatening rain finally appears."

Over the next few days Christopher tried to recapture the excitement he had been feeling over the work he was doing at Hawkings, but even instituting the desperately needed repairs to the most dilapidated cottages on the estate and the gratifying response of the pensioners who lived there failed to lift his spirits. He'd been looking forward to these renovations for years and now the savor had gone out of it.

Precisely one week after their first visit, the carriage of Mr. and Mrs. Winterbottom once more appeared on the drive. This time Christopher was waiting for them in the grand salon, an array of delicacies laid out on the table and fresh tea in the elaborate silver tea pot.

"I'm afraid Caroline is still unwell," he said as he came forward to greet them. "I would have sent word, but she insisted I give you her regards in person since you were so keen to drive all this way to visit her. Cake?"

The couple looked momentarily nonplussed, but in the face of Christopher's bland assumption that they would follow his lead, they allowed themselves to be seated and accepted refreshment. Country visits were of necessity longer than the fifteen minutes' duration deemed adequate in town. But to Christopher this one seemed to drag on without end, due in equal measure to the stilted conversation on Mr. Winterbottom's part and the inane utterances of his wife. When the pair finally rose to take their leave, he was astonished to realize only a single hour had passed.

Christopher escorted them to their carriage with alacrity and had just raised a hand in a casual wave when a snippet of wind brought the voice of Winterbottom back to him from inside the confines of the carriage.

"There you see, my love, nothing to worry about. You can write to your sister and tell her all is well."

Christopher had no idea what the words meant and cared even less. With a final wave, he returned to the house and prepared himself for another afternoon and evening of work and solitude, glad that chore, at least, was behind him.

Four days later he received a letter from his sister that both explained the cryptic utterance and ignited his temper.

My dear Christopher, it read, *I feel I must warn you of a most ridiculous rumor spreading like wildfire amongst the more thoughtless members of the* ton. *It appears someone—no, don't get into a pet because I'm not naming names, I truly do not know—anyway, someone has been vaunting it about that after a terrible quarrel you have done away with Caroline and are now trying to conceal that fact. Of course most people recognize how absurd it is. After all, if you were going to do away with her in order to inherit her money, which has also been suggested as one possible motive since—who knew!—she is (was) fabulously wealthy and that's the only reason you married her in the first place, why would you conceal her death? And of course, why you would need to do away with her to get at her money since you are her husband—well, not really, but you know what I mean—and therefore entitled to anything she might possess, is not explained. And if you killed her in a jealous rage or some such nonsense why did no one hear a cry for help, or at least the quarrel that preceded the dreadful deed? And where on earth is her body? I make light of it, but indeed it is an unpleasant situation in which to find oneself. Of course, no one with any sense believes anything of the kind.*

You will not wish to pay for a second sheet and I know how you hate it when I cross my lines, so I will leave it here. Be assured I will do everything possible to get to the bottom of this ridiculous misunderstanding and shall keep you informed.

Yours etc.
Eleanor

When he'd finished reading, Christopher's first instinct was to rip the expensive piece of stationary in two and consign it to the fire as its contents so richly deserved. But that wouldn't change anything. Slamming down his coffee cup, he got up from the breakfast table, where he had been reading his post over a thick slice of ham and an assortment of buttered rolls. He knew very well from where the ridiculous rumor had arisen, and he cursed the entire Winthrop/Winterbottom clan to perdition. This, then, was the explanation for the apparently nonsensical statement he had overheard the other day as his unwanted guests had driven away. No doubt Clarissa had done exactly the opposite to what her husband had advised and immediately written to her sister a tissue of lies and insinuations about Caroline's suspected whereabouts that would have put 'Monk' Lewis, the famous author of the most lurid fantasies imaginable, to shame. It wouldn't have taken long for the two of them to concoct a tale as improbable as it was pernicious and then delight in how quickly it spread.

It probably hadn't taken more than a day or two for them to start believing it themselves.

Chapter Seventeen

Caroline, sitting in the parlor of her great uncle's house in unaccustomed stillness, listened to the rain as it beat against the window behind her. The letter she had received that morning from the lawyer lay almost forgotten in her lap, and she wondered at her complete lack of excitement. Her dream was about to come true. She had fulfilled all the requirements of her great aunt's will and now had the means to go forward with her horse breeding facility. It was something she had been planning for, been dreaming about, for so long and now there was nothing and no one to stand in her way. It didn't seem fair that it had turned to ashes because of something so trivial as a broken lock and a man who seemed to be constitutionally incapable of minding his own business.

No, that wasn't fair either. It wasn't the fault of the lock or the interfering man that she had fallen in love. Or that her love was not reciprocated. She couldn't even blame Christopher, much as she'd like to in the darker hours of the night. One didn't love at the wish of another. One didn't love because it was convenient to do so. One didn't love at anyone's behest. One just did.

And one didn't stop loving at anyone's behest. Not even one's own. And that truly wasn't fair. Fortunately, as she told herself firmly and repeatedly, Caroline didn't expect the world to be fair. If it was, she wouldn't have lost not just one, but both her parents at so young an age that she didn't even have a few memories to cherish. And, she allowed, if it was, she wouldn't have spent her entire life fed and sheltered and wanting for nothing, without having earned even one of the myriad of advantages she took for granted on a daily basis. When one thought of all the poor and desperate children there were in the world whose only crime was the circumstance of their birth, that certainly didn't seem fair.

She straightened resolutely, determined to take full advantage of the enviable position she found herself in. She would succeed, she told herself, and she would take both pride and satisfaction in that success. And if she lived out her life alone she would still be luckier than ninety-nine percent of the people who inhabited the earth.

She went over to her desk, which had been installed in the parlour as a compromise with her uncle between having an actual office, which is what she would have preferred, and sitting in lady-like idleness, which is what her uncle half-heartedly believed young ladies were meant to do. He had tutted unhappily at its installation, but as she had pointed out, since she was the only young lady with whom he was acquainted, he had to take her word for what would be suitable and not just rely on what he had occasionally gleaned from absentmindedly picking up a copy of *Ackermann's Repository*. He had seen the logic of her argument and toddled off to his own book-lined study and the magnificent desk behind which he spent most of his days.

As well as the desk, Caroline had recently had a

bookcase installed to hold her breeding manuals. Her uncle might not allow her to have an office of her own, but he would soon find that the parlor was starting to look remarkably like one. Pulling a ledger off a shelf, she sat down to plan out her initial requirements and estimated expenditures.

She was barely ten minutes into her task when the housekeeper poked her head around the door and said in a voice that sounded vaguely scandalized and in a tone that exemplified the familiarity that servants of long standing felt they'd earned: "Miss Saxon, there's a young man at the door who says he's come all the way from London to see you. He looks like a ragamuffin to me, but he insisted you know him. Says his name's Westmore. Should I send him packing?"

"Michael!" Caroline jumped up from her desk, all accounting and planning forgotten. "Don't be absurd, Hannah. You wouldn't send a dog packing in this weather, as well you know. What can have brought him here? There must be something dreadfully wrong."

She hurried through the door and out into the foyer where she found Michael manfully attempting to stop himself from dripping all over the marble floor.

It was an impossible task. He was clearly soaked to the skin. What water wasn't pouring off his hat and greatcoat was dripping steadily from the end of his nose.

"Caroline," he exclaimed when she appeared, squelching forward and then coming to a rather shamefaced halt. "I'm sorry. I'm afraid I'm rather wet. It's raining outside."

"It looks like it's raining inside as well," the housekeeper, who had followed in Caroline's wake, muttered.

"Hannah, go and get some towels for Mr. Westmore at once," Caroline instructed, worry sharpening her voice. "Michael, come into the parlour and tell me what brings you here. Is everything all right? Christopher isn't..." her voice trailed off.

"Christopher's fine," he assured her as he followed her obediently into the room. "So's my mother. Nobody's dead or anything, not yet, anyway. It's just, well, we need your help." He stood dripping hopefully, watching her face.

"Of course." The response was instant and automatic. "But we must get you out of those wet clothes before you catch pneumonia. Have you brought a change of clothing? I'll have someone take you upstairs where you can dry off. I'll be right here when you come back down again."

She paused, her sapphire eyes widened with apprehension and her voice just a little tremulous. "But, Michael, you do promise that Christo...everyone is all right?"

"Yes, I promise," he said instantly, as he followed a servant back out the doorway before ominously continuing. "At least for now."

Containing her worry over Michael's mysterious appearance at her door by attending to the practical matter of welcoming an unexpected guest, probably a very hungry unexpected guest if she knew anything about young men, Caroline immediately arranged for a substantial tray of food to be sent up to the parlor. She slipped into the library to inform her uncle that a guest had arrived and managed to overcome his curiosity about her relationship to the young man by implying he was travelling around Ireland looking at horses and had promised to look her up if he were in the neighbourhood.

She loved her great-uncle Tobias dearly, but had not seen the necessity of divulging to him the radical change in plans that had marked a very different London season from the one they had originally envisioned. It would have just complicated things to no advantage and her rather unworldly uncle would probably have been as confused by her explanation as he was by the bewildering information he found in the perplexing pages of women's magazine. Depending on what Michael had to say, that decision may need to change, but for now she was happy to keep him in ignorance.

Her judicial choice of words convinced him there was no need to personally greet the young man who had appeared so suddenly at his door. After asking Caroline to covey his hope they would meet at dinner, assuming the young man stayed long enough to dine, he happily returned to his books and musings.

Her duties fulfilled, Caroline composed herself to wait for Michael's return. Fortunately, she did not have to wait long. Before many minutes had passed, a very different creature came through the parlour doorway than the one that had initially washed up on the doorstep. Dried, brushed, and reclothed in what Caroline had to admit was record time, Michael grinned at her exuberantly when he saw the stack of pies, breads and cheeses she had arranged for, not to mention the steaming pot of coffee.

"I say, Caroline, that looks like just the thing. It's amazing how hungry one gets just sitting on the back of a horse getting more and more wet and miserable, but not really doing anything."

"Yes," she said, gesturing him to a seat at the small table and trying to contain her impatience. "I thought you might need refreshment after your journey. Help yourself."

Needing no second invitation, Michael piled a plate with as much food as could reasonably be considered to not cross the line into outright gluttony, and dug in enthusiastically. He had not, however, failed to notice the pallor in Caroline's cheeks or the way her hands were clenched together in her lap, so after apologizing for speaking with his mouth full, he began his tale.

"Of course it all started with Annabelle Winthrop. What a deuced nuisance that girl is! I remember what she was like when we were growing up. All simpering and listening at doors. Wouldn't play cricket in case she got her dress dirty, but always ready to carry tales about what the rest of us were up to."

Despite her apprehension Caroline couldn't help but laugh. "I hadn't realized you were that close to each other."

Michael shot her a look of horror over a mouthful of pork pie. "I should say not," was the somewhat muffled reply. "She's two years older than me in any case, but you can't help but run into people when you all live in the same neighbourhood and visit the same houses."

It wasn't a world Caroline had much familiarity with, but she was happy to take Michael's word for it.

"What has Miss Winthrop done?" she prompted.

"Pretty much ruined everything." Michael swallowed what looked like half a wheel of cheese before continuing. "For some reason she got it into her plaguey head you were having an affair with Robert Waverly and has been telling just about everyone she can buttonhole about it."

"Captain Waverly! And me?" Caroline's eyebrows shot up. Her voice was a full octave higher than her usual deep tones. "That's absurd. No one could believe such a thing. And surely it doesn't matter, whether people believe it or not. They'll soon have something more dramatic to talk about. That cannot be what brought you here."

"Well actually it does matter. And it's quite remarkable what people will believe when they set their mind to it and someone speaks convincingly enough. We once had the head of college completely convinced that Borden, a great friend of mine, was a girl in disguise just because we kept calling him 'her' and then looking guilty. When he found a dress in Borden's closet it was all we could do to dissuade him from having him stripped down to his unmentionables in the middle of the quadrangle." Michael paused, a look of wonder coming to his face. "Come to think of it, we might have done him a favour. By the time the old man had been convinced of Borden's true sex, he'd forgotten about the dress and how it came to be in Borden's digs in the first place. Dashed lucky. But that's neither here nor there, of course," he added hastily.

"But why would Miss Winthrop say such a thing? And why would people believe her?" Caroline was as bewildered as ever.

Michael looked somewhat abashed. "Well, people talk, don't they? When they've nothing better to do. My mother tells me there were rumors going round that you and Christopher weren't as close as you used to be. Then Annabelle was at some ball or other and out on the balcony—where she had no business being, I might add!—and saw you and Waverly disappearing into the bushes. According to her he had his arm around you and the two of you were discussing what a villain Christopher is before disappearing into the shrubbery. Not a word of truth in it, of course," he hastened to add before stuffing another piece of meat in his mouth.

Caroline thought back to the evening of the Duchess of Chatterton's ball. Christopher had been so cold to her and Captain Waverly's kind attention, as well as his knowledge of her situation, had been so soothing. She tried to remember their conversation. Had one of them really called Christopher a villain? She couldn't remember doing so, but it was the kind of thing easy to make up or, to be more charitable, misinterpret. She and Waverly had walked down the steps into the garden. She remembered that clearly. They had been seeking more privacy, but the path had been well lit. Lady Chatterton was not a woman to put up with anything havey-cavey going on in her grounds. It had been a relief to talk to someone who understood Christopher in a way that was completely different than the perspective of a doting older sister. Of course he hadn't put his arm around her, but someone intent on a little malicious gossip would have no difficulty embroidering that small damning detail onto the fabric of the tale.

"Well, I hope I don't need to tell you I'm not having an affair with Captain Waverly," Caroline managed to say in her usual calm tones. "But I can just about see how someone with too much imagination and much too little common sense might convince herself something was going on between us." She told Michael quickly about the Chattertons' ball.

"But surely a bit of gossip isn't going to hurt us now. It might be a bit uncomfortable for Christopher, but that's all. Let them say what they wish."

Michael's worried expression hadn't cleared. "It's not that simple," he burst out as soon as Caroline finished speaking. "After spreading that complete rasper around town, Annabelle got it into her head to enlist her sister into the mix. No sooner had Annabelle told her what she suspected than Clarissa must be off to Hawkings, dragging that fool of a husband of hers with her in order to get to the bottom of things."

"But there is no bottom of things to get to!" Caroline protested.

"Well, there wouldn't have been if you were there," Michael agreed. "But you'd already left to come here. Christopher fobbed them off with some tale of you being ill, but that just made things worse. Their busybody staff, who ought to be taught to keep their noses out of their betters' business, informed their mistress you hadn't been seen since you first arrived at Hawkings and people were beginning to wonder what had happened to you. Most were quite content to be told you had taken ill, but not Clarissa and Annabelle. Until Waverly turned up in town last week and assured everyone he'd just been to Leicester to see someone about a horse, they had it bandied all about that the two of you had run off together and Christopher was just trying to save his pride."

"Good God." Caroline rose from her seat and

agitatedly started to pace the room. "You can't be serious. Those women are a menace. But surely no one in their right mind believed them, even before Captain Waverly's reappearance."

Michael looked uncomfortable. "Well, there were too many people who'd seen how cold you now seemed with each other. And they started remembering that they didn't really know much about you."

"And, of course, where was I?"

"Well, yes," Michael agreed, a pink tint rising to his cheeks.

"But why is there a problem now? Everyone must admit I haven't actually run off with Captain Waverly. Does that not put the gossip to rest?"

Michael's mouth twisted, as if reluctant to say the words he knew he must. "Not exactly. You see, the Winterbottoms, that's Clarissa and her husband, went back to Hawkings a week later and you still hadn't been seen and Christopher still insisted you were too ill to receive any company and Clarissa made it her business to discover that neither the doctor nor the parson had seen you..." He took a deep breath and continued all in a rush. "And now it's too late for your original plan to work. If you're suddenly declared dead, I'm quite convinced Christopher may be arrested. You must come back before they hang him or chop off his head or whatever it is they do to peers who've been convicted of murdering their wives!"

Chapter Eighteen

Several days after receiving the letter from Eleanor, Christopher once again heard the sound of carriage wheels on the drive. He had been trying to get some work done in his study, but hadn't been able to concentrate. He almost welcomed the interruption, and wryly wondered whether things had come to such a pretty pass that the constabulary was now at his door and demanding answers.

When he walked outdoors to greet his visitors his first thought was that the constabulary would have been a welcome alternative.

He didn't mind Eleanor, who looked up at him coming down the gray stone steps as she exited the carriage with a curious expression of apology on her face. It was the person whose trembling and imperious hand demanded Eleanor's help negotiating the few small steps that had been let down for her descent from the old-fashioned barouche in which the pair had travelled that made him stare.

"Mrs. Winthrop." He stepped forward and helped her the rest of the way out of the carriage, his words stilted and his tone belying the words. "This is an unexpected pleasure."

She cackled up at him—there was really no other word for it—as they slowly climbed the stairs to the front door.

"I'll not lay my best bonnet on it!" she said. "'What the devil is this old harridan doing on my doorstep?' is what you're really thinking, I'll be bound. Well, get me inside by a warm fire and I'll tell you."

Since this was exactly what Christopher had been thinking he was at a loss how to respond. "Not at all," he replied rather inanely.

Eleanor, a few steps behind, snorted, and Mrs. Winthrop's attention was immediately diverted.

"In my day, no lady would have dreamt of allowing such a noise to emanate from her person," Mrs. Winthrop said sternly. "That's half the problem with the world today. No sense of decorum."

"I'm sure you're correct," Christopher said, ushering the old lady through the door. He glanced over his shoulder at Eleanor, a look approaching desperation on his face.

"Sorry," she mouthed and shrugged, clearly indicating she had no control over the situation.

It was well over half an hour later before the ladies, refreshed after their somewhat difficult journey—one because of her age and the other because of the company—were comfortably seated in the drawing room. Mrs. Winthrop, waving the teapot away with a look of deep disgust on her weary face, demanded a glass of brandy 'for restorative purposes.'

After taking a long drink and smacking her lips in satisfaction she finally turned to Christopher and barked, "I suppose it would be completely useless to ask to see your wife."

"I'm afraid so," he replied, allowing no emotion to appear on his face.

Mrs. Winthrop nodded in apparent satisfaction.

"Thought so." She leaned forward, trembling hands crossed on the elegant ebony cane that accompanied her everywhere, her eyes bright and shrewd. "She's no more taken to her sick bed than she's sprouted horns and a tail."

Eleanor, who had been watching Christopher doing the polite to the old lady with a slight smirk, gasped.

"She's left you, hasn't she?" Mrs. Winthrop's laugh sounded more like a cackle than ever and she was obviously unmoved by Christopher's chilly reception. "I assumed that's what had happened when Clarissa told me she and that buffoon she's shackled to had been turned away at the door."

"They were hardly turned away, ma'am. My wife was simply indisposed."

"Ha! She wouldn't be the first bride to be indisposed. Indisposed to another place altogether, I wouldn't be surprised. There's a good deal of adjustment to be made in the first year of marriage and it isn't always easy. Especially for the men. Caroline's a woman of spirit. I can see her taking umbrage if someone tries to lay down the law in a way she doesn't like."

Christopher stared at her for a long moment before finally saying, "My wife's character is not the issue. Though I appreciate your concern, if that's what it is, I fail to understand what has brought you to Hawkings. Our problems, if we have any and I'm not saying that we do, are no bread and butter of yours."

"Well that's where you're wrong. Don't think I'm not aware it was that idiot granddaughter of mine who started the whole thing. Just like her father as far as brains are concerned, but without his good nature."

Mrs. Winthrop seemed little concerned with the slander she'd just spoken about her own firstborn. "A bit of gossip is one thing, but when it starts to impinge on someone's reputation to the extent that serious damage is in the offing, it must be stopped. So I'll ask you again and give me the word with no bark on it. Has Caroline left you?"

Christopher looked toward Eleanor in wordless consultation before shrugging and replying simply: "Yes, she has." It was the truth after all, no matter if the old termagant put a completely different interpretation on it.

Mrs. Winthrop nodded in satisfaction. "Thought so. Well she'll be back, but in the meantime we've got to stop this from going any further before they throw you in prison or worse, completely rip your reputation to shreds. Do you know where she is? I don't suppose there's the slightest hope of you going after her and bringing her back."

"No," was the short reply.

Mrs. Winthrop nodded again. "Didn't expect you to say anything different. You young people with your megrims and tempers. You'll get over it and your marriage will be all the stronger for it, but while you're in the throes, everything's a crisis of Herculean proportions. In the meantime, we must try to tamp down a few fires."

Mrs. Winthrop was basing her conclusions on incorrect information—at least their real deception hadn't become public knowledge. Then the fat would really be in the fire. Nonetheless, Christopher couldn't stop himself from asking, "Why are you so sure she's not having an affair with Waverly? What makes you think she'll come back to me?"

The response was swift and unexpected, accompanied by a snort she would have vehemently condemned in any other female. "Just because I'm old doesn't mean I've completely lost my senses and that includes my sense of sight. I've seen the way the two of you look at each other. Don't make me laugh. Of course she'll come back. Besides, she's a sensible woman even if it weren't a love match, which it obviously is."

Christopher stared at the ancient little Tartar ensconced in his living room with her twisted hands clutching the handle of her cane, but her back resolutely straight and the fire still alight in her eyes. Her words both startled him and gave him hope. He laughed for the first time in days.

"Mrs. Winthrop, you're a treasure. But I really don't think you needed to have come all this way. Things will sort themselves out, I'm sure."

"Given the opportunity I dare say you're right. But you may not get the opportunity." She waved her hand at Eleanor with all the imperiousness of a Stuart monarch commanding one of his more minor minions. "Show him the newspaper."

Eleanor obediently reached into her reticule and extracted a folded piece of paper that, judging by its quality and the particular font of the writing with which it was covered, had been cut from the Morning Chronicle. She handed it to Christopher silently.

How quickly things change! it read. *Has it only been a few months since the* ton *was delighted and surprised by the sudden marriage of Lord S. and a MYSTERIOUS Irish beauty he met while travelling abroad? Many a maidenly heart was frustrated by the removal of such an eligible* parti *from the marriage mart, but the newlywed couple's clear affection for each other was a beacon of hope for those extolling the virtues of marital bliss.*

It seems, however, that things were not as they seemed. A SERPENT looks to have been lurking in their garden of paradise and its hissing whispers are now being heard in all the best drawing rooms. Everyone is asking! Where is Lady S.? She is reportedly infirm, but NO ONE can affirm the truth of the matter. No one has seen her. Not a doctor. Not a midwife. Not a clergyman. Yet all visitors are turned away. Is she truly ill or is that just a clever deception? Has she run off with ANOTHER? Or is there a more sinister explanation?

Lord S. says nothing. How long will it take for the authorities to start asking questions about the sweet young dove entrusted to his careless hands? Why do they do nothing? How can a lady disappear with no consequences? Why should a lady be allowed to disappear simply because she seems to have no family to look out for her and demand an accounting? Justice must be done; society's rules must be followed by the highborn as well as the low and this question must be answered: WHERE IS LADY S.?

For a moment he thought he was actually seeing red as the anger built inside him. He knew, he had always known, how barbed were the circles in which he moved. That knowledge had led to this whole charade in the first place. Nonetheless, such a piece of tripe as he now held in his clenched hands brought it home to him with much more immediacy than Eleanor's letter had done. The thought of everyone twittering and whispering with such venal glee about something that should be private, and about Caroline, who had never done anything to deserve such treatment almost made him sick.

He stared at the words without really seeing them as he composed himself. It took several minutes before he turned his eyes away from the page and looked steadily at Mrs. Winthrop.

"What must we do?"

The skin around her eyes crinkled and the thin line of her ancient lips tilted ever so slightly upwards. "That's a question I don't get asked nearly often enough."

"And I'm sure the world is worse off as a result," Christopher interjected, a bit of the good humor she had unexpectedly invoked returning.

She snorted again, clearly not ill-pleased and trying not to show it. "None of your bamboozling, my lord. I was learning to see through the likes of you long before you were born or even thought of." Her protests fooled no one.

Amused or not, Christopher was about to ask her what possible help she thought she could be when a discreet noise behind him made him turn his head. Branston stood in the doorway, his expression bland enough to give the impression that no thought had ever gone on behind it or was ever likely to in the future.

"Mr. and Mrs. Winterbottom have called, my lord," he informed them.

"Well, send them packing!" Christopher said immediately. "Surely you don't need me to tell you that."

"Bring them in at once," Mrs. Winthrop said at the same time. "They both need a good talking to."

Branston enacted a stately bow in her direction, acknowledging her words, before continuing to speak to Christopher. "I'm afraid, my lord, that Mr. Winterbottom says he is here on official business and will not be deterred." If a slight hint of distaste crossed the butler's face it could only be seen by the most discerning eye. "I do not presume to know what Mrs. Winterbottom's presence indicates, but I did not consider it seemly to leave her standing on the doorstep whilst ushering her husband in."

"No, of course not," Christopher said with a hint of impatience. "Show them both in."

"Exactly what I said," muttered Mrs. Winthrop to no one in particular as Branston bowed himself out of the room.

It was clear from the expression of bright expectancy on her face as she swept through the door that Clarissa Winterbottom anticipated participating in one of the most enjoyable experiences of her short and shallow existence. The plummeting of expectation was matched only by the drop of her jaw when she saw who was sitting in pride of place on Christopher's best settee.

"Grandmama!" she squeaked. "What are you doing here?"

"Trying to tidy up the mess you and that idiot sister of yours have made before things get a good deal worse," Mrs. Winthrop snapped. "What the devil are you doing here?"

A variety of expressions flitted across Clarissa's face—horror, consternation, shock and a *soupçon* of titillation—before she remembered her original purpose and the puerile glee returned. "I'm here to help my dear

Winterbottom arrest Saxon!" she said, brightly as her husband stepped through the door behind her, clearly horrified by her words.

Chapter Nineteen

"No, no, my dear! You mustn't say such a thing."

His words, however, were largely ignored by the three inhabitants of the room.

"How dare you!" Eleanor cried, springing up from where she had been seated in a chair next to the settee and glaring at Winterbottom.

"Don't be absurd," were Mrs. Winthrop's contemptuous words. "I'm quite sure you have no idea what you are talking about, you pea goose."

Even Branston gasped audibly before closing the door behind the uninvited and unwelcome guests.

Christopher, eyes narrowed, was the only one who said nothing, and it was to him the hapless Winterbottom turned.

"My lord," he said with a good deal of deference and a just a touch of intractability. "I wonder if we might speak in private somewhere."

"You can wonder all you like," Christopher responded. "What I wonder is why you think you have the right to make such a request, and why you and your wife have seen fit to pay me yet another visit."

Winterbottom hesitated as his wife scurried over to claim a seat on the settee with Mrs. Winthrop. "Oh, grandmamma, you can call me a pea goose all you like. I know your funning ways. But I assure you I know exactly what I'm talking about." She sat down as if prepared to regale her aged relative with all the details, paying no heed at all to either Eleanor's outraged expression or the feelings of the subject of her tittle tattle, who remained standing firmly where he was, eyes never leaving Winterbottom's face.

"Well?" he asked, gently.

"No, my lord," Winterbottom said frankly. "Not well. But the fact is, since I bought my little estate here, I'm the magistrate for this county and it's my duty to ask you some questions. There's no getting around it." He seemed to swell as he spoke. Embarrassed though he might appear, he clearly reveled in the authority the role invested him with. "Now we can have our little chat here in the drawing room with these ladies watching or we can repair to a more private venue. If I were you I know which I'd prefer, but it's entirely your decision." Seemingly of their own accord, Winterbottom's shallow blue eyes skittered toward the settee where his wife was leaning confidentially toward her grandmother, a gloved hand held up to conceal her mouth as if she had suddenly grown some discretion.

Christopher found himself at a loss. He had no wish for a private conversation with his self-important new neighbor, who was clearly destined to become a blight on the county. But nor did he care to hear what the man had to say, or be forced to answer his questions, in front of his gloating wife.

"You may have ten minutes in the library," he finally conceded. He opened the door and bowed. "After you."

The library, with its cracked leather chairs and welcoming walls of books, had always been a favorite room of Christopher's, at least until he spent so many hours sitting at the large desk by the window trying not to think of Caroline. He saw Winterbottom's gaze turn longingly toward the table in the corner that Branston always ensured was well stocked with a selection of brandy and port, and took a shallow pleasure in ignoring the man's obvious desire. He took even more pleasure in strolling over to lean one elbow on the mantel and place a foot on the broad hearth. If the intruder insisted on speaking to him, he could damned well do it without a glass in his hand or a chair to sit on. No matter how much it might go against the grain, Christopher was quite prepared, was quite happy in fact, to offer no hospitality whatsoever.

"What do you want?" His tone was as abrupt and unwelcoming as he could make it without actually being rude.

"I think you know why I'm here, my lord."

"What I think is apparently of no consequence or you wouldn't keep appearing on my doorstep. If this isn't *another* social call, which it obviously isn't, say your piece and be done. As you can see, I have guests." Christopher pulled the watch which hung on a long chain out of his pocket and looked pointedly at it.

Winterbottom drew himself up to his full height. "Very well, my lord. I am here to inquire into the disappearance of Lady Saxon."

"And just why do you think she has disappeared?"

Winterbottom's mouth dropped. He looked shocked at such a disingenuous question. "Come, come, Saxon. No one's seen her in weeks. Where is she? What has become of her?" Winterbottom tried to sound reasonable and failed miserably.

"No one's seen a good many people in weeks. That

doesn't mean we run around in a meddlesome frenzy trying to discover their whereabouts." Christopher's voice was contemptuous. "I believe my wife has as much right as anyone to a degree of privacy and to not have her every move scrutinized by a bunch of busybodies who should be minding their own business instead of everyone else's."

"Of course she does," Winterbottom promptly replied. "No one's denying that. But questions have been raised. An official request has been made to investigate and it's my duty to do so."

"Do what you must then." Christopher snapped his watch shut. "You'll get no help from me."

Winterbottom bowed with rigid dignity. "That, of course, is your privilege. However, I must warn you that if no trace of Lady Saxon can be found, it will put you in a very precarious position. A very precarious position indeed. Are you sure you do not wish to reconsider?"

"The only thing I'd like to reconsider is my initial welcome to you and your wife in the first place. Without your officiousness and your wife's…well, let's be gentlemanly and call it inquisitiveness, I wouldn't have been put into a position where I have to defend my movements or those of my wife." He stepped away from the fireplace, his eyes cold. "I find I have no need and no desire to grant you ten minutes after all. Allow me to see you to the door."

"My lord…"

Christopher spoke softly. "I strongly advise you not to threaten me again, magistrate or no magistrate, or we'll see just how far your powers truly extend."

"Very well, my lord," Winterbottom answered.

"Let us hope that you don't come to regret this."

Christopher strode to the door. "You'd be better served ensuring your own position is safe, rather than worrying about mine."

He turned the knob and wrenched open the door to discover Branston standing outside it, one hand raised to knock and eyes wide in consternation.

"What the devil are you doing out here?" he asked, patience worn thin.

Branston stepped back and collected his dignity. "I'm sorry to interrupt, my lord, but I felt you should be informed despite your desire for privacy. Captain Waverly has just arrived. I've taken him into the salon with the ladies."

Winterbottom forgotten, Christopher crossed the hallway to the salon. He didn't know what had brought his oldest friend to Hawkings and wasn't sure whether to expect the best or the worst. It had been that kind of day. The house was getting fuller by the minute, and he didn't know how many more intrusions he could stomach.

When he entered, Mrs. Winthrop was still sitting on the settee being regaled in an excited whisper by her granddaughter with just what outlandish tale Christopher could only imagine. The look on the elderly lady's face almost made up for a lot of what Christopher had been forced to endure by the younger woman's husband.

Waverly and Eleanor stood by the window, heads together, faces serious and voices lowered. It appeared more than one confidence was being shared.

Winterbottom, who had followed Christopher into the room, motioned urgently to his wife several times and was just as determinedly ignored.

"Robert?" There was a note of guarded enquiry in Christopher's voice as he spoke from just within the doorway. "To what do we owe this pleasure?"

Waverly looked around and an expression of conspicuous cheer crossed his face. "Christopher," he cried. "I was just telling your sister. Caroline's all settled and feeling much better. I promised her I'd reassure you first thing."

"Did you now?" Christopher asked, one eyebrow raised.

Eleanor jumped in. "You know how upset she was that you weren't able to escort her to Scarborough yourself. But now she's feeling a little better, she realizes how unreasonable she was."

"Scarborough!" Winterbottom exclaimed.

Eleanor turned to him, wide-eyed. "Yes. Didn't Christopher tell you? She wasn't feeling well, as I believe you and Clarissa were informed when you paid your first bridal visit. Or was it your second? Christopher finally persuaded her to take the waters, but he was unable to accompany her because of some...repairs he needed to see to." She laughed, smoothly injecting a trace of embarrassment into her voice. "I'm not sure what it was. Something came up. You'll have to ask him." She turned to her brother. "Why was it you couldn't escort Caroline, Christopher?" she asked brightly.

"I hardly think it matters to our guests or would be of the slightest interest to them. Suffice to say I did not do so." Christopher, not quite sure what was going on, but certain some scheme or other had been quickly dreamt up, kept his contribution to the bare minimum.

"Fortunately, I was heading in that general direction and was able to step in as Christopher's replacement," Waverly interjected blandly. "I say, Christopher, I came through town on my way back and there are some absolutely appalling rumors running around. You wouldn't believe the things people say. Not just say, but actually seem to believe."

"Wouldn't I? You'd be surprised," Christopher growled.

"If Lady Saxon has simply gone to Scarborough on a cure, why did you not just tell me in the first place?" Winterbottom asked, still sounding suspicious.

"Because it's none of your business." Mrs. Winthrop spoke for the first time. "I'm surprised you haven't both been thrown out on your ear coming in here with your nasty suspicions and gossip mongering. I'm heartily ashamed of both of you." She turned to Christopher. "My lord, allow me to apologize."

Christopher stepped forward and took the hand she held out to him in his own. "There's absolutely no need for you to do so, ma'am. It appears your visit was unnecessary, but I'm grateful you came all the same. You're looking tired, if you don't mind me saying so. May I escort you up to your room?"

Mrs. Winthrop, who had indeed been sagging a little, straightened. "Thank you, Saxon, but I'm not completely done yet. I believe that instead of taking any more advantage of your hospitality I'll accompany Clarissa back to her home. We need a good long chat. Come along, girl. I believe we've bothered these good people long enough."

Clarissa looked anything but thrilled by the idea, but she had long since learned not to argue with her formidable grandmother. She started collecting herself to leave.

Winterbottom, however, seemed to be made of sterner stuff. He was on the trail of a possible felony, and was not prepared to let go of the bit that easily.

"Are you saying you escorted Lady Saxon to Scarborough?" he asked Waverly, who looked down his nose at him.

"I don't believe I've had the pleasure," he said.

"This is our new neighbor, Mr. Winterbottom," Eleanor informed him. "He's a magistrate."

"That's no reason for him to be questioning my movements as far as I can tell," Waverly answered.

"Yes, he does seem to be fond of asking questions he has no business asking," Christopher said. "He seems to think it's his duty. You might as well answer. The sooner you do the sooner we'll be rid of him."

"Very well then. Yes, I escorted Lady Saxon to Scarborough so she could take the waters. I left her there improving enormously after promising to inform her husband of her continued progress." He turned to Christopher. "I've got a letter for you, by the way. Remind me to give it to you when we've a moment's peace."

Winterbottom still wasn't convinced. "There've been some nasty rumors abroad, rumors concerning you and Lady Saxon. It all seems highly suspicious to me. I thought so from our very first encounter."

Christopher had had enough. "That does it. As you can see, Captain Waverly and I are on the best of terms. Would that be the case if the rumors you allude to were true? I've had enough of your insinuations and accusations. For the last time, my wife is in

Scarborough. Now please leave my house before I have you forcibly ejected."

Clarissa jumped up from the settee and Winterbottom, eyes wide and finally convinced, backed toward the doorway hastily only to stop abruptly as his bulk encountered the door frame. He turned and gasped as he beheld another person who had jumped back in alarm as he attempted to blunder his way out of the room.

"Good heavens, what on earth is going on here?" a deep whiskey voice asked, and was met by sudden silence.

Chapter Twenty

Winterbottom fell back and Caroline entered the room with every appearance of composure. Despite the overwhelming assortment of people who seem to have assembled in the Hawkings best salon, her eyes immediately focused on Christopher. All thoughts of the other occupants had vanished, along with her equanimity. He might as well have been the only person in the room. She stepped toward him as if her very volition had been taken from her. She had no idea she had moved.

"Caroline." Her name came out as more a caress than speech. In Christopher's voice it became an invocation. A supplication. A prayer. She was only a few steps into the room before he met her, his motions as instinctive as her own. He took her hands in his, grasping them as if to assure himself of their reality. Slowly he lifted them up to his lips, his deep dark eyes gleaming as he drank in the sight of her.

No one had ever looked at her that way before. She had never thought anyone would ever look at her that way. As if she were desirable. As if she were the most important thing in the world. As if she were the only reason for existence. It was heady stuff. Who knows how long they would have stood in the all-encompassing world of each other's gaze, had their reverie not been cut short? A cane was being banged persistently on the carpeted floor.

"Well, the girl's not dead. Not in Scarborough either, which probably amounts to the same thing. I can't abide watering holes and never could. Nasty places with foul-tasting water and even worse company." Mrs. Winthrop stood up and tilted her head at a regal angle, the more effectively to stare down her nose at Christopher and Caroline. "I expect you two to sort things out and start behaving properly. Any more scandal will certainly be on your own head and nothing to do with me or mine. I'll see to that. So you can't rely on me to step in again and tidy things up. I've had enough careening about the countryside." She suddenly looked old and tired. Christopher, with a smile that started in his eyes and travelled all the way through Caroline's body, reluctantly released her hands and turned to his erstwhile champion.

"Mrs. Winthrop, you are indeed a wonder. I'm truly grateful for your help and understanding."

"And now you wish me to the devil. Well, quite right. Come along, Clarissa, and for God's sake close your mouth before you catch a fly. Winterbottom, you may give me your arm." Ignoring the rest of the inhabitants of the room, she tottered toward her startled but obliging grandson-in-law and swept out under his careful escort. Now that Caroline had inexplicably returned, it was clear he relished the opportunity to leave the premises as quickly as possible. Clarissa, trailing in their wake, threw an apologetic, slightly scandalized look over her shoulder before following obediently out the main entrance where the ever efficient Branston stood holding the door open.

Caroline, who on the journey to England had been

regaled with the story of Clarissa's interference in what should be their private affairs, was human enough to hope she worked herself into a frenzy trying to understand what was really going on between her and Christopher. One thing she was certain of was that, thanks to their formidable grandmother, neither Mrs. Winterbottom nor her sister would be spreading any more rumors.

"Gosh, what a Tartar!" Michael had been standing quietly in the hallway watching the drama unfold with every evidence of enjoyment. "I wouldn't like to get on her wrong side."

"Michael!" his mother exclaimed, noticing him for the first time. "What are you doing here?"

Indignation stormed into his face. "I should think that would be obvious. Pulling Uncle Christopher's fat out of the fire. I've been on the road pretty much forever going to Ireland to bring Caro..." He suddenly noticed Captain Waverly leaning against the mantel, arms crossed and an amused expression on his face. "That is I..." He stopped short and sent an appealing look to Caroline.

"It's all right, Michael," she said, glaring at Christopher, who seemed too amused to come to his befuddled nephew's rescue. "Captain Waverly is aware of our arrangement. You can speak freely in front of him."

"Indeed you can," Waverly said. "I salute you, Michael. Of course, I'd already dispelled the crisis by telling that jumped-up toad I'd escorted Caroline to Scarborough. I'm sure they're now completely confused by the whole thing. Nonetheless, you stepped into the breech like a gentleman and that's what's important."

"Just a minute," Eleanor interjected before Michael had a chance to retaliate. "While we're grateful, of course, for your attempts on our behalf, we were working out a perfectly feasible plan to get out of this mess."

"Well if it didn't involve Caroline, I don't see how you were going to manage it," Michael said. It was clear he was put out by how little his efforts seemed to be appreciated.

"Well at least it was conceivable. Now she's here looking fit as a fiddle, I don't see how you're going to kill her off without causing a great deal of talk indeed." Waverly was not going to give up the credit so easily. "If she downed a vial of poison in front of half the *ton* after declaring her intention to kill herself, they'll be sure to blame Christopher somehow, all the while muttering about smoke and fire."

Identical expressions of dismay crossed the faces of mother and son.

"Good God," Michael exclaimed, turning to his uncle. "You're going to have to marry her after all."

"Don't be absurd." Caroline could feel the heat rising to her face as she spoke. This was a catastrophe.

"It really does seem to have come to that," Eleanor said gently, as Captain Waverly nodded his agreement, a slight smile tilting the side of his lips.

Caroline turned to Christopher in wordless entreaty. Surely they were being ridiculous. But his attention was not on her. He was frowning, perhaps glowering would be a better word, at his dearest relatives and closest friend. "Thank you all. It's quite clear that without each and every one of your efforts

217

both singly and in concert we would have been in grave trouble, er, graver trouble. Now if you'll allow me five minutes alone with my…with Caroline, we'll do our humble best to live up to the sterling example you've all set and see if between the two of us we can sort a way out of this sorry mess."

"But Christopher…"

He walked to the door and held it open firmly. "Go on. You've had your chance. Now it's my turn." Meekly the three conspirators departed.

Caroline did her best to keep her tone even and her voice collected. Christopher's reaction to her sudden appearance had certainly thrown her, but she had been misled before. She couldn't allow herself to hope. "Well, I must say, my lord, it's a very good thing you hadn't already set it about that I was dead, or I wouldn't have been able to reappear so handily. Though the situation is bad now, it surely would have been worse then." She suddenly found that keeping her voice steady was harder than she had expected. "But I must admit I don't really understand why you've delayed it these weeks."

"Can't you?" Unlike her, Christopher seemed to have no trouble with his voice. It was warm, the tone intimate. "Well, thanks to the best of intentions on the part of a group of people I could happily strangle at the moment, my reasons for doing so have become irrelevant. But can you not guess what they were, my clever Miss Saxon?"

Caroline was having a difficult time thinking at all with Christopher standing so close and looking at her in such a way. She was in no position to guess anything and softly shook her head.

"I had every intention of following you to Ireland and asking for your hand properly," he said, taking the object under discussion in his own and lifting it once again to his lips. "However, I wanted to make sure you had been given time to settle back into the life you had planned and make your decision based on your feelings alone. Therefore I delayed any announcement concerning your health and well-being. I couldn't say anything that would prevent you from returning to society if, as was my dearest hope, you consented to make me the happiest of men."

Caroline shook her head, unconvinced, applying her mind to the problem and trying to still the rapid beating of her hopeful heart. "But, why? If you...if you care for me, why did you not say so in all the time I was living under your roof?"

"Because you were living under my roof! My God, what sort of cad would take advantage of a woman in such a way? I wanted you to come to me willingly, not because you were afraid of ruin or because you felt some sort of obligation. Not even because you might have been swept off your feet by the circumstances in which you found yourself. The only true test of love is whether it is offered freely and that could only be done from the safety of your own home." For the first time the gentle tone left his voice. He sounded shaken and unsure. "Trust those with my best interests at heart to damn near ruin everything."

Caroline suddenly remembered Michael's words and any gladness she felt seemed to turn to stone. "And now that very thing you dreaded is happening. Only it's you who faces ruination if we don't marry, not me."

"No!" Christopher took her by the shoulders, his

gaze intent, no hint of a smile on his face. "I will not allow you to be coerced. If you refuse to marry me, we'll simply tell the world we're separated. They were happy enough to think our marriage was in trouble. Eventually we'll go through the motions of getting a divorce. You'll have long since left to get on with your life, and I really don't give a damn what society chooses to believe about us. Let them turn me into a social pariah. I will always have Hawkings. To hell with London. I'm sick to death of it. This must be your decision, freely made."

Caroline looked at him uncertainly. Something in his eyes, something that went beyond desire to a deeper, richer place swept her apprehension away. Her lips tilted upwards and her sapphire eyes met, unafraid, his dark troubled gaze as she said, "But no one's given me a decision to make."

Christopher's brows drew together as he tried to parse her meaning and then his expression cleared. "My dear, practical Miss Saxon, for no practical reason whatsoever, will you be my wife, truly and forever more?"

"Not because either one of us is ruined?"

"Certainly not."

"Not to save you from going to jail?"

"If the answer is no, then jail's as good a place as any to spend the rest of my days, but no, not that either. Simply because I love you to the depths of my soul."

"In that case, my lord, I will marry you, for I find my soul is in a similar state." She raised her face to his in time to be swept into an embrace that she felt to the centre of her being. When Christopher's lips touched hers, it was as if her mouth had only been created for the purpose of receiving his. She returned the kiss with fervor, with a feeling of rightness that she knew would never leave her. She tightened her arms around his neck, pulling him even closer. She had found her home, and it was in Christopher's arms.

****

After all the gossip and speculation, it was a bit of a nine-day wonder when Lord and Lady Saxon departed on another honeymoon. But by the time they returned there were plenty of other reputations lying around and simply begging to be ripped to shreds. And besides, what could really be said about a couple who insisted on practically living in each other's pocket? Really, it wasn't at all amusing. Which, as Mrs. Winthrop wasn't shy to point out, was just the way it should be.

A word about the author...

Barbara Burke's peripatetic life means she's lived everywhere from a suburban house in a small town to a funky apartment in a big city, and from an architecturally designed estate deep in the forest to a cedar shack on the edge of the ocean. Everywhere she's gone she's been accompanied by her husband, her animals, and her books.

For the last ten years she's worked as a freelance journalist and has won several awards. She was a fan of Jane Austen long before that lady was discovered by revisionists and zombie lovers and thinks Georgette Heyer was one of the great writers of the twentieth century.

She lives by the philosophy that one should never turn down the opportunity to get on a plane no matter where it's going, but deep down inside wishes she could travel everywhere by train.

Thank you for purchasing
this publication of The Wild Rose Press, Inc.

For questions or more information
contact us at
info@thewildrosepress.com.

The Wild Rose Press, Inc.
www.thewildrosepress.com